Writers' Anthology Group

Alpha and Omega

Alpha and Omega

All rights reserved. No part of this book may be reproduced, stored in a retrieval system, or transmitted, in any form or by any means without the prior written permission of the publisher, nor be otherwise circulated in any form of binding or cover other than that in which it is published and without a similar condition being imposed on the subsequent purchaser.

First published in 2014 by Bent Banana Books in association with the Writers' Anthology Group.

Visit bentbananabooks.com.au

Visit www.artsalliance.org.au

Bent Banana Books *email bentbananabooks@gmail.com*
24 Lorraine Court Lawnton, Australia, 4501.

Phone 617 3264 2311
Email peter@petercampbellrealty.com
Web www.petercampbellrealty.com

A CiP catalogue record for this book is available from the Australian National Library
ISBN 978-0-9872784-1-8

Cover graphic and design, Ken Armstrong

TABLE of CONTENTS:

FOREWORD BY BERNIE DOWLING

ON behalf of the Writers Anthology Group, based in the Pine Rivers district of Australia, I present our 2014 anthology, *Alpha and Omega.*

This anthology follows three critically acclaimed volumes published by Bent Banana Books in conjunction with the Arts Alliance Pine Rivers. These anthologies were *The Writing on the Wall* (2010) *Can You Believe It* (2011) and *Sweet and Sour* (2012). Last year, Writers' Anthology Group (WAG) produced *Serendipity.*

Again we have short stories and poetry, illustrated by local artists, mainly photographers.

Some writers and illustrators have been with us from volume one; others are newbies; we thank all for their contributions.

Authors range from people who earn or have earned a living from writing to those being published for the first time.

This year we are proud to include the winners of the inaugural Peter Campbell/ WAG Literary Awards. Paimarire Teague, a Year-11 student from Dakabin State High School, is the gold-medal winner and Tatiana Werle-Bertling, a Year-12 student, also from Dakabin State High School, won the silver medal. I commend their stories to you.

This year's title *Alpha and Omega* has inspired a diversity of short stories and poetry.

Our collective of writers and illustrators has produced a quality book without undue financial burden on any of our 20 or so writers.

We acknowledge the work of our editorial panel: Bernie Dowling, Vera Murray, Anne Olsson, Lorraine Noscov, Ronald Holt and David MacLaughlin, as well as that of our cover designer/ illustrator Ken Armstrong.

We warmly thank our corporate sponsors Peter Campbell of Peter Campbell Realty, based at Albany Creek and Morayfield, and Bent Banana Books of Lawnton.

Now, let the adventures begin.

– Bernie Dowling, *WAG editorial committee*

WE ALL MEET IN THE STARS

Phil Devine

IT was October, 2009 – The International Year of Astronomy. I found myself sitting beside my telescope which I had set up on the Council Chambers lawns in the heart of Alice Springs and, truth to tell, I was feeling like a bit of a dill.

The International Astronomical Union supported by UNESCO had decided to commemorate the 400th anniversary of one Galileo Galilei, a professor of mathematics at the University of Padua, first pointing the newly invented telescope, (or spy glass, as it was then named) at the heavens above. That year of 2009 would be declared the International Year of Astronomy. Hereinafter I will refer to it as the IYA. Galileo's sightings of the moons of Jupiter, the phases of Venus and the heavily cratered surface of our own Moon would usher in what can only be termed as a scientific and philosophical revolution, the perturbations of which are still being felt today.

Galileo did not invent the telescope but he most certainly refined it from the fairly primitive instrument as it first appeared. Nor was he actually the first individual to point it heavenwards. He was beaten to the punch by several individuals including the Englishman Thomas Herriot, an Elizabethan scholar and tutor to Sir Walter Raleigh. It was however Galileo who first published his observations in his book *The Starry Messenger* and thus stole the thunder from any pretenders to the throne.

All talk of scientific and philosophical revolutions aside, I was still feeling like a bit of a dill. Please allow me to explain.

Part of the commemorations of the IYA was to encourage amateur astronomers and stargazers to set their telescopes up in public places around the world and then invite the public to take a view of the greatest show on Earth – the glorious heavens – in a practice which is often called 'sidewalk astronomy'– a practice first initiated by the Vedantic monk, John Dobson. Dobson believed that anyone who owned a telescope was under a moral and spiritual imperative to share the view through the eyepiece with those who did not own a scope.

Dobson was a most remarkable individual and is well worth Googling. He devised and designed a type of telescope, now known as a Dobsonian, which was large in aperture, cheap to make and easy to transport. His superiors in the monastery, noting his predilection for building telescopes and lurking the streets at night on his sidewalk astronomy missions, eventually felt obliged to ask him to leave.

I had already in my limited way attempted to discharge my Dobsonian duties by inviting friends, neighbours, work colleagues and acquaintances out to my home some 20km SW of Alice Springs to show them what I could of the revolving Universe above. This was the IYA though and special efforts were required. Although not a member of the local astronomical society, I had been invited to participate in their version of sidewalk astronomy. So it was that one Friday night in October, I loaded all my kit into the back of my ute and headed into the light-polluted skies of the township of Alice Springs to spread the light of astronomy.

I got there early before anyone else had turned up and selected what I thought was a suitable site on the Council lawns, just opposite one of the local watering holes. It didn't take long to set up and once done I sat at my small table which held my star maps and binoculars and settled in with a Thermos of coffee. Normally I enjoy an ale or two with my observing, but as I was acting as a public ambassador of the gentle art of stargazing, I was feeling strangely moral. The smell of alcohol on my breath might not be entirely appropriate.

For those of a technical bent, my scope is a 12-inch diameter Newtonian reflector on a Dobsonian mount (yes, the same Dobson). For those not so inclined, it looks like a large household electrical hot water system sitting on a cannon mount. So there I'm sat, beside a hot water system, painfully sober and out of my comfort zone on the Council lawns on a Friday night, waiting to show people the wonders of the Universe and wishing I was elsewhere. And you wonder why I'm feeling like a bit of a dill.

In the meantime some of the members of the astronomical society turn up and start setting up their gear. There's a bit of introductions and discussing of gear before everyone settles down behind their scopes. Great! *At least I'm not a dill on his own*, I think to myself.

It's starting to get dark.

I look up and see a bloke and his girlfriend regarding me suspiciously from the footpath. I feel like an Irish bomb-maker who's just been caught at his craft.

'Do you want to see the Moon?' I say, in an attempt to justify my presence there.

'How much?' he asks.

'Nothing,' I say. 'It's free.'

This seems to decide them and they wander over. I sight the scope and line it up on the Moon and then stand back to let them have a look. They think it's great! They take turns for a while, exchanging excited comments. It's obvious to the three of us that they've got value for their money. I'm slightly emboldened now.

'Do you want to see Jupiter and its moons?' I ask.

In the spirit of nothing ventured, nothing gained, they decide that they will. Again, they're visibly impressed. *This is going quite well*, I think to myself. It's just like showing my friends out home; it's just that I don't know these people. We chat for a bit and I answer some questions about the scope and they decide that they have to get going but might come back later.

I notice some more people loitering on the footpath regarding me curiously. The P. T. Barnum in me is slowly emerging. 'Come and see the wonders of the Universe,' I call to the three or four curious onlookers gathered. They wander over.

The astro society has picked a good night. Being a Friday, everyone is out and about; Jupiter is riding high in the eastern sky and the Moon is at a partial phase meaning that its light isn't overpowering dimmer Jupiter. Also the Moon is at a suitable phase for discerning its myriad craters.

I suddenly realise that a queue has formed behind my scope. I look over at my compatriots at their scopes and see that they are doing similarly well. People are excited – they're having fun, seeing things they've not seen before and the only cost is a couple of minutes of their time. It's a feature that I've noticed before in crowd psychology – emotions are contagious. The more people that are having fun, then the more fun there is to be had by more people. It's a weird exponential effect that affects me as much as it's affecting my clients. The more cheerful and excited that they become, the more cheerful and excited that I become. I realise that I've been lining up the scope for people for over an hour now and I've actually done little to no observing myself and I really couldn't care less. This is bloody great!

I'm regaled with questions, some of which I can answer, some that I can't.

How far away is the Moon? About a quarter of a million miles. *How far away is Jupiter?* Not certain. I know that the light of the Sun takes about 45 minutes to get there.

How big is the Universe? No one knows for sure.

How did it all form? Where did it all come from? Lighter elements like helium and hydrogen were subjected to unimaginable pressures and temperatures and condensed down until the process of nuclear fusion took place and ignited into burning spheres that we call stars. Particularly heavy stars condensed to such a state that they percolated heavier elements like carbon and iron. The American astronomer Carl Sagan took great delight in pointing out that such stars exploding with unimaginable force scattered these heavier elements throughout the universe until they coalesced and accreted into planets such as our own Earth. We are all made of star stuff. (Apologies to any astro physicists who read my simplified explanation here.) *Are you a scientist?* I laugh. No, I'm just an interested bystander.

We are all made of star stuff. That really blows them away.

One of the characteristics of Alice Springs is that we are a tourist town and as such it is possible to meet people from all over the world in our humble streets. I'm reminded of this several times during the night. A Japanese girl and her boyfriend are next.

They speak English about as well as I speak Japanese but commonality of language is oddly enough not a requirement at the viewing end of a telescope.

I line up the Moon for her and stand back. Scarcely has she gazed through the eyepiece when she lets out an ear-piercing shriek that would put an Irish banshee to shame. She literally runs on the spot gesticulating wildly to her boyfriend amidst much excited lingo which I can only assume means something along the lines of: 'This White Devil has cooked up some serious magic in his hot water system. Best you look too and make sure that he has not possessed me in some nefarious manner!'

The boyfriend regards me with not a little suspicion but decides to go boldly all the same. He looks and also starts back from the scope. He says nothing but gives me a strange glance all the same before taking another look. They chatter excitedly to each other and the girl takes another look. Again the shriek. I look about nervously to see if there are any police in the immediate vicinity. The coast, fortunately, is clear. They continue chattering to each other, taking turns at the eyepiece. At last they've had their fill and, both smiling, they bow ceremoniously to me. I smile and bow back. It seems to be the least I can do.

A German woman is next. I show her Jupiter and its moons and then our own Moon.

'Ahh,' she sighs, 'In Germany we cannot see the stars!'

The excitement of the young Japanese couple suddenly falls into context, but I'm also outraged on her behalf. Can't see the stars! Can't see the stars!! It's our birth right to see the stars! I am familiar with the insidious effects of light pollution even in our own cities in Australia but it takes a simple wistful statement from this European woman to bring home to me the extent of this tragedy.

Can't see the stars? May it never, never happen here!

I spend a little extra time with her and show her a couple of globular clusters – densely packed balls of millions of stars that constitute some of my favourite viewing targets.

I look around at the queue and next up are some of the local 'Boys in da Hood' – young indigenous males, cocky and self-assured. Not going to be easy to impress these lads.

'Can we have a look too?' asks the first bloke in line. I'm immediately taken by his polite manner and his obviously genuine curiosity.

'Course you can, mate,' I say, swivelling the scope about for each of them in turn.

They all have a go and it's obvious that they have been impressed. As they head off, one of them claps me on the shoulder and says, 'Thanks for that, Chilpie.'

Chilpie is an Indigenous word that means 'old man' but it doesn't have any of the pejorative meaning that the same phrase might have in English. It translates roughly as 'Elder' and is actually an address of respect.

But it's one of the last viewers of the night that really makes my evening. An Indigenous woman in her mid-twenties approaches me.

'I want to see the Moon,' she announces without preamble.

I move and focus the scope and stand back.

Now, usually when someone looks into the eyepiece there is an almost simultaneous verbal expression of wonder or enjoyment. The young Japanese lass was something of an extreme at one end of the scale, but nevertheless people are usually moved to say something. In fact, a common Australian expression of Anglo-Saxon biological coupling leads me to suspect that for many people, viewing through a telescope is an act of almost sexual connotation.

But from this girl, there was nothing. Not a sound.

I waited a little while and then thought that perhaps the rotation of the Earth had caused the target to move out of the focal plane of the eyepiece. My scope doesn't track targets automatically like the computerised ones do. So I asked if she could still see the Moon; did she want me to realign the scope?

Still nothing.

Damn! This isn't going at all well, I thought.

It was then that she turned from the eyepiece and from the street lights across the street I could see two streams of tears coursing down her cheeks.

'That's beautiful,' she said in a shaking and husky voice.

Tears filled my own eyes. 'Yes,' was all I could manage quietly. 'Yes, it is.'

'My people have so many stories about the Moon, but none of them have ever seen it like this. They should all see it like this.'

With that, she turned on her heel and was gone, taking most of my heart with her.

It was getting late. Most of the people who had been out on the streets were now in the places that they had been headed to before being rudely interrupted by the sidewalk astronomers. No one would be out again until the pubs started to empty. By mutual agreement we sidewalk astronomers began to pack up to go home.

As I drove my ute out along the dark country road that led to home, I gazed out the side window at the glorious stars shining above me and I thought of the many people I had met that night. I thought of the excited little Japanese lass, the wistful German woman and especially the Indigenous woman who had moved me in a way that I had never before been moved. I thought of Dobson's admonishment to share my telescope and I thought of Sagan's aphorism that we are all made of star stuff and unbidden, something arose from the depths of my own mind.

Yes! We all meet in the stars!

The Alpha and the Omega
Anne Olsson

The end lies in the beginning; the beginning rests in the end.
For there is nought to seek, and nothing to defend.
The seeker must stop seeking, the finder will always find,
But only in the silence, and never in the mind.

The truth it lies within, and is always to be found,
Not mired in illusion but in the depths profound.
When shadows fall on life, the ego seems triumphant,
But a false sense of self reveals itself redundant.

When all fear drops away, 'tis needless to be brave.
There is no 'you' to guard, there is no 'you' to save.
When you escape your prison, when all is seen as One,
When mind is not the master, the ego is undone.

So let the Heart speak for you, and still the restless mind,
And peace will find a welcome, and sight will greet the blind.
For there is nought to seek, and nothing to defend.
The end is in the beginning, and the beginning is in the end.

VISION III

FLIGHT OF THE RELUCTANT PSYCHIC

Jane Sharp

EARTHBOUND

Jane Sharp

AS she drove along the back roads of the Sunshine Coast Hinterland, Trudy Harper relished the mildness of the winter weather in Queensland. The day had started out cold and misty but the sun was starting to break through and Trudy thought she would be able to take her jumper off by midday. Having not long moved into the area and because she was her own boss, she had decided to go for a drive to get to know her surroundings. Moving to the country had been a part of embracing a new life after the heartache she had suffered since enduring personal losses. This time last year she had been a police detective with the Metro Major Crime Squad, now she was beginning a new career as a practising psychic.

As she thought about her most recent loss, that of her younger brother, his spirit appeared in the passenger seat next to her. His unexpected arrival made Trudy jump.

'Shit Josh! Do you have to do that?'

Josh laughed. 'Lucky you're wearing your seatbelt or you'd have hit the roof.'

'I see being dead hasn't made you grow up,' said Trudy.

'Hey, you of all people should know that death doesn't magically turn someone into a saint.'

'What do you want Josh?'

'I popped in to let you know that I've been assigned to your guardian team. Apparently I need some spiritual growth or something. I'm also supposed to tell you that there's an old track coming up on your right in about two minutes' time. You should turn down there and see what happens.'

'Why?' said Trudy.

There was no reply. The passenger seat was once again empty.

A short time later and with no clue as to where she was going or what she was going to find when she got there, Trudy turned her bright orange Jeep onto the overgrown track. If Josh had not told her about its existence she would have driven right past the entry without even noticing it was there. The track wound through bushland that looked like it might once have been cleared for use as farm land. Up ahead on the left, Trudy saw the ruins of what once was a timber farmhouse. The walls that had supported the roof had crumbled, leaving the rusty sheets of corrugated iron to lie haphazardly where they had fallen. The front wall still stood like a facade from a movie set.

Trudy stopped her vehicle in front of the ruins.

Before getting out she did a meditation of psychic protection the way she had been taught to do by her friend and mentor Elise Schembri. She always felt ridiculous when she did the little rituals that Elise assured her were necessary safety precautions. With an attitude of better to be safe than sorry, Trudy finished what she was doing and approached the derelict building. On closer inspection it looked as if there had been a fire at one time.

After entering the front yard Trudy was glad that she had protected herself. Something unseen attacked her and attempted to break through the diamond-like barrier that she had mentally constructed around her to use as a shield. Her unknown attacker tried from every direction to penetrate the protective barrier. There was a brief pause before Trudy felt the attack come from overhead. Fortunately she had been thorough and had shielded herself completely, even the soles of her feet.

The attack stopped abruptly and was followed by the sound of a woman crying. Breathing deeply, Trudy closed her eyes and opened them slowly. She saw a woman standing near the old front door of the house. The woman was wearing a floral, shirtwaist dress. Trudy thought that she looked like a housewife from the 1960s.

'Hello,' said Trudy. 'Can I help you?'

'You can see me?'

'Yes.'

'I wasn't trying to hurt you but I'm stuck here and desperate to get out.'

'If you look around you, there should be something to show you the way out. It could be a tunnel or a gate, or maybe even a bridge.'

'I know where the gate into the afterlife is, you stupid cow,' the woman snapped at Trudy. 'I don't want to go there.'

Surprised by the spirit's attitude Trudy ignored the impulse to leave the woman to her misery and asked her, 'Where do you want to go?'

The woman looked at Trudy with greed in her eyes and said, 'I want to get away from this damned farm. I want to smell the flowers and feel the wind on my face. I want to taste wine and food again … and ice-cream too. I want to live the life I should have had.'

'Why didn't you,' asked Trudy.

'Because I married a stupid hick to get away from my parents, and then he got himself conscripted into the army and sent to Vietnam. He left me here.'

'He didn't come back?'

'He did, but he found out that I'd been unfaithful and left again. What was I supposed to do? I needed help here and I got lonely. My lover showed me that there was more to life than rotting away on some old farm.'

The woman drifted off into her memories. 'We had some great parties here, with lots of booze and groovy music. My boyfriend had a lot of cool friends that liked to get away from the city and they loved to come here to hang out.

'When we heard that my husband Dennis was coming home Rory moved back to the city. I was hoping to convince Dennis to move to the city but the bloody town gossips got to him first and convinced him that I was a slut.

'Anyway, we had a massive fight and he told me he would stay in town for a couple of days and that he expected me to be gone by the time he came back. That night I drank half a bottle of rum, smoked a joint and passed out. I woke up to the place on fire around me. My first thought was to try to escape until I realised I was standing looking at myself on the bed. It was too late. I watched my body burn but I didn't feel it. I knew I was dead but I wasn't ready to go. It's so unfair. I should have moved to the city while he was away and found someone else to take care of me.'

'Or you could have taken care of yourself,' said Trudy.

The woman ignored her, 'I never got to wear a mini skirt. Or a pair of those gorgeous white lace-up boots. You know, the shiny ones made from patent leather.'

'It doesn't sound like you were forced into anything. It seems to me you made your own choices and manipulated other people,' said Trudy.

The woman approached Trudy and said, 'I apologise for trying to take over your body. You're the first person to come along since I worked out a way to escape, who's been anywhere near suitable. Kids come by now and again on a dare. The last thing I want is to be inside some pimply teenager. I don't want to go through growing up again. You're a little bit older than I was but at least you're an adult and female. I just want to have a taste of what I missed out on. Can't you just let me pop into you for a short time?'

Trudy shook her head. 'That would be a big fat no. Once in, you'd never leave.'

'You could stay, just scooch over a bit. You could be in charge.'

'Once again, I'll say no. There's no way I'm going to open myself up to being possessed. We both know you would eventually try to take over.'

The spirit pouted and stamped her foot like the spoiled brat she was.

'I thought you wanted to help me,' she said.

'I do but not at my expense. Besides, just because it's what you want doesn't mean it's what you need.'

The spirit rolled her eyes.

'What's your name?'

'Catherine,' the woman told her.

'Catherine, every life has a beginning and an ending. You know, A to Z, Alpha and Omega. Our physical lives are finite but our spirits aren't. I think the afterlife is actually where we go to sort out what we do next. I call it the in-between because I don't think it's the ultimate end. Your attachment to the material world is holding you back and you've become trapped. All those things you miss about being alive, well there's a good chance you'll get to experience them again. There might be something else even better to take their place. The longer you stay here the harder it will be for you to move on and as time passes you'll become more resentful.'

Some of the aggressiveness seemed to leave the woman. 'I'm scared,' she said.

'Because you did things you weren't proud of?'

The woman nodded.

'I don't know exactly what it's like over there, I do know there's no need to be scared. Once there you'll gain knowledge and insight to help you to find your way. There are others who can offer you guidance. You won't have to work it all out on your own. If you stay here you'll stagnate and leave yourself open to evil. You could find yourself on a very dark path.'

The woman thought for a while, 'Will you come with me? Not all the way, I know that's not possible, but can you come part of the way?'

Trudy studied the other woman's spirit. She seemed sincere. Aware there was a possibility that she was being tricked into leaving her body, Trudy reinforced her psychic shield and called on her guides for their protection and help. Sitting down on the overgrown footpath leading to the house Trudy made her first ever attempt at astral projection. After visualising a mirror image of herself sitting opposite, she concentrated on moving her conscious mind over to it. There was a creaking sound as her consciousness left her physical body. Once out she was surprised to find that she had no body at all. She had been expecting to find herself in an ethereal version of her familiar body. At first there was a weird feeling of only existing as an awareness until slowly a subtle body began to take form around her conscious being. There was a silvery cord joining her astral body to her physical one.

'Elise is going to be so pissed when she finds out how easy this was for me,' thought Trudy with a smile.

As with most of the paranormal practices that she was learning, things that were supposedly difficult to do came easily to Trudy. It looked like astral projection was no different.

Trudy saw Catherine make a sudden move towards the now vacant shell of the physical body that had slumped onto the ground. A few centimetres from the dead woman's goal a sparkling wall appeared and blocked her path. Trudy could see Josh and an elegant woman standing before it. Josh pushed the angry spirit away.

There was a shimmer and the world became overlayed with another. Trudy could see the vague outline of her Jeep occupying the same space as a rickety, wooden bridge. On the other side of the bridge, figures were beckoning to the spirit of the woman.

'NO! I won't go. I don't want to. You can't make me.'

Trudy looked over at Josh.

He nodded and said, 'She's right. We all have free will. It's the most important thing there is. A soul can only be ready to take the next step, when the next step is what that individual truly wants to do. You can't force her to crossover.'

'Then what was the point of all this?'

'It's also important to try,' said Josh.

A figure separated from the crowd on the opposite side of the bridge. He stopped in the centre of the bridge. He was wearing Army greens and a slouch hat and Trudy guessed him to be the woman's husband from her previous life. He held out a hand to the woman.

'Come on Catherine, it's not so bad.'

'There's no life over there,' said the woman petulantly.

'How do you know? It's just different that's all. With time and patience you'll get used to it. You just have to let yourself.'

'But I don't want to be with you.'

'You don't have to. No-one will make you do anything you're not ready for. I came across for you because I'm probably one of the few people you trust. If you want to stay earthbound that's your decision, but nothing is going to change for you until you make peace with the choices you've made.'

All the fight seemed to go out of Catherine and she started to weep. Trudy went to her and hugged her. Then hand in hand the two women walked silently towards the ghostly soldier. He gently embraced Catherine but she pushed him away and turned to smile at Trudy. In that smile Trudy thought she saw a hint of apology and perhaps some gratitude. Trudy returned the smile and raised her hand in farewell. The spirit couple walked calmly across the bridge where they were enveloped by the crowd of waiting spirits.

Trudy felt a thump. There was a brief moment of blackness and disorientation. When she opened her eyes she was back in her physical body and the world had returned to normal. The spirits were gone and the bridge to the in-between no longer lay over the Jeep. Looking up at the sky Trudy noticed how heavy her meat body felt.

'Meat body...hahaha...good one Trudy,' she thought.

Josh appeared next to her as she sat up.

'Nice work Sis,' he said.

'I didn't really do much,' said Trudy.

'You did enough,' said Josh. 'See ya' later Sis.'

He was gone before she had a chance to say goodbye, Trudy shook her head and got to her feet.

The ruins of the farmhouse looked the same but the air around it felt different. Getting into her Jeep to begin the ride home Trudy thought about how this kind of thing was becoming a regular part of her new normal. Turning the car around she headed back the way she had come leaving the empty farmhouse behind her.

THE ONE ABOUT THE FARMER'S DAUGHTERS
Bernie Dowling

Middle of nowhere, 75km from Birdsville, Queensland, September, 1993.

THE radiator hose hissed at me like a punter encouraging a fast racehorse or discouraging a bad comedian. Steam swirled from the hose raising the air above beyond its previous 40-degrees temperature. In disgust I slammed my cheap straw hat into the red dust.

For three hours I sat, listening to the radio, in the driver's seat of the motionless EH Holden ute. Both doors were open and a plastic bottle of warm water kept me company. The radio played wailing country music.

The country station answered my begging for a decent song by playing the 1985 Talking Heads ditty *Road to Nowhere*.

The high excitement of my first trip to the annual Birdsville horse-racing carnival had sustained me over 1500 kilometres. That was the distance I had travelled from my humble home in the Brisbane suburb of Hendra. Every serious Australian punter was expected to make, at least once in their lifetime, the trip to way out in western Queensland, on the edge of the Simpson Desert. There is the Queensland Outback and then there is Birdsville. The racetrack is no Royal Ascot. The prizemoney is nothing flash. Punters have been forever flocking in their thousands for the annual Birdsville races 'just because', an addiction hard to break when you cannot even classify it.

I looked skyward. The descendants of the birds which gave the town its name were nowhere to be seen. A few metal birds had flown overhead carting the early birds of the 6000 people set to join the 100 citizens of Birdsville for the races. It was Thursday and the races were on Friday and Saturday. I wearily noticed dusk perched above the highway and contemplating a plunge.

The Japanese four-wheel-drive, which pulled up behind me, wore more dust than the bush highway. The driver climbed from the cabin but he could have stepped from the pages of Australian history, or at least a Hollywood version of it. He was mid-40s, tall and thin. Beneath the pristine Akubra hat, his confident face was as red as the dust at his feet, except for his chin's sandy stubble, neatly clipped but untamed by a razor.

He wore a Jackie Howe, a navy singlet, evenly coloured, unstained and creaseless, under an unbuttoned short-sleeved denim shirt. Beneath that were pressed moleskins and polished leather boots, with red dust surreptitiously creeping up the edges of the soles. He told the teenage girls, both pretty-faced blondes, to stay in the four-wheel-drive. He strolled towards me. 'Have an accident?' he asked.

'No thanks, just had one,' I said.

'Thought so.'

He looked at me, stared into my eyes actually. I looked at his blue eyes briefly before lowering my glance.

'Better get you home,' he said.

'I live in Brisbane.'

'Hnnh, don't suppose you have a tow rope.'

'Not on me, no.'

'Hnnh, thought so.'

He drove the 4WD to park in front of the ute, took out an ancient thick grease-stained rope and hitched the two vehicles together with some pretty fancy knots. He returned to his driver's seat, beside the teenagers, who might have been smiling at me but were more likely smirking. He started his engine, killed it, and returned to the ute.

'You know to put it in neutral?' he said.

'That's how I got here,' I said.

He stared into my eyes again and refused to blink before he finally spoke. 'You say the stupidest things. I'll put it down to sun stroke.'

The farm house was 15 minutes down bush tracks after we turned off the highway. The house was three times as long as it was wide, verandas all round, the exterior off-white in colour, tinted ochre over the years by dust.

Inside was spotlessly clean — high ceilings, hallways leading to lots of rooms. A delicious smell rode the heat haze from the kitchen. In the bush, many still have dinner before dusk, after a hard day's yakka on the land.

The girls, who looked to be in their late teens, smiled at me from tanned faces set with blue eyes. Everybody but me had blue eyes; I had to make do with grey. The young women took plates from a cupboard and cutlery from a drawer to a solid rectangular wooden table in the middle of the large kitchen. The dining room, beside the lounge, was empty of furniture, empty of everything, actually, except space. Eight wooden chairs, with padded brown leather seats, pushed against the durable kitchen table.

The man looked across at me and nodded towards the head of the table. Not sure what he was indicating, I stood still. He shook his head, moved, and roughly pulled out the chair to the right of the head one. Having finished laying the dinner ware, the young women gently withdrew chairs, one to the right of me and one opposite. Neither girl sat down. I realised they had not said a word between them. I wondered if they were mute.

The man pulled out his chair at the head of the table and the three of them waited for me. I sat down. They sat down.

I tapped the impressive table with a knuckle. 'What sort of wood's this?'

The man looked warily at me. 'Ironbark.'

'There is worse wood to have a bite on,' I said.

He ignored that. 'You can wash up before tea,' he said. 'If you don't mind wasting water.' Tea means dinner in the bush, though it also means the beverage. After a couple of decades in Australia, new chums understand most of the lingo.

'I'm sweet,' I said. 'I'll just end up dirty again.'

'Hnnh,' he said.

The blondes went to the stove and placed hot food from two saucepans into large ceramic dishes. One opened the oven and brought out a loaf of hot bread which she placed on a plate.

Using a ladle one blonde motioned to place its contents on the man's plate. He pushed a palm towards the ladle. 'Him first.'

I inhaled the aroma of rich beef stew as the blonde held the ladle before me. 'You're not vegetarian, are you?' she inquired sweetly. Ah, she speaks. Perhaps the other one does too.

The man answered for me. 'Course he's not. Does he look vegetarian? How tall are you? About six foot, I reckon.'

'About that,' I said.

'You're skinny, but that's probably drugs, not vegetarian food.'

You know how in the movies someone says, 'I don't like your tone', but no one ever says it in real life. I didn't like his tone. But I did not say it.

I stared down at my plate covered in large chunks of beef surrounded by onion rings, diced carrots and thick gravy.

I smiled gratefully at the blonde who moved to serve the man. The other blonde came to my side to put large portions of mashed potato, mashed pumpkin and boiled peas around the edge of my plate. We nodded at each other as she moved towards the man.

The four of us soon had our meals including side plates of buttered hot bread. The man nodded at me and I ate. They ate.

'How far are we from Birdsville?' I asked.

'Haven't been there for years,' he said.

I looked at the girls who tittered. The so-far-speechless blonde opposite me obviously had the gift of sound.

'They haven't moved it since you were there last, have they?' I said.

I heard both girls take in breaths.

'You're a real joker, Mr Steele Hill,' he said.

'You know me.'

'I looked at your driver's licence while I unhitched the tow-rope. You should keep it in your wallet not in the glove-box of your car.'

'Then you wouldn't have found it.'

'Might have.' He threw my licence across the table.

The girl nearest me tapped my forearm.

'We are the Graves. Dad's George. My sister's Isobel and I am Francine.'

Nods all round.

'As you know, I'm Steele.'

I tapped the table again. 'Ironbark and Steele, made for each other.'

Francine and Isobel laughed politely but George hung tough.

'You did that one already.'

I was going to correct him but instead put my hands out in a gesture of misunderstanding.

'Ironbark and Steele, it's the same joke as having a bite on Ironbark. Dogs bark and they bite.'

I looked at him to see if he was serious. I had not implied any connection between the table and a dog. It would have been clever of me to do 'ironbark and bite' but I could take no credit for it. The way it was going down with my toughest audience member, I would not want to.

I had little opportunity to appease George Grave before what he said next startled me. 'You calling my family dogs?'

'No, I didn't mean any of that. My jokes are very shallow,' I said.

'Shallow Graves, now.' He thumped the table with his fist and his daughters exchanged concerned looks. 'We didn't have to stop for you,'

George Grave said.

He had me worried, no doubt, but the thought that he had spoken gravely caused a tiny smile at the edge of my mouth. I really needed to stop finding humour at inappropriate times.

'I know you didn't have to stop,' I said solemnly. 'And I'm glad you did. I've driven all the way from Toowoomba and the ute's packed it in. I was just trying to lighten things up.'

'Toowoomba, you said you were from Brisbane.'

I may have said that but now I did not want him to know where I lived. 'I thought you might not know where Toowoomba is. So I said Brisbane.'

'Hendra's a suburb of Toowoomba?' he asked. 'Hendra, that's what it says on your licence.'

'Yes,' I said. 'I mean no, Hendra is not a suburb of Toowoomba. But it does say Hendra on my licence.'

I waited. He looked at the daughter on his left and back at me.

'Only been through Toowoomba twice, quite a while ago. Only been to Brisbane twice and never been to the horse races.'

'Every Australian should go to the racetrack at least once,' I said. 'If you are ever in Toowoomba, I'll take you to Clifford Park.'

'Might keep you to that when I visit Isobel, like I keep promising.'

'Visit Isobel?'

The blonde on his left answered for him with a smile. 'I am studying drama at Toowoomba Uni. Second year, I have been living in the City of Flowers for eighteen months.'

For some reason, I felt I was on the middle of a tense protracted hand of cards, playing poker.

'That's right; it's uni holidays, isn't it?' I said. I discreetly wiped a bead of sweat from my left eyebrow and looked to my right. 'What about you Francine, you studying in Toowoomba?'

Francine put her knife down and rested her chin on one fist. 'Fraid not,' she said.

I deserved this consolation.

'I am studying law at the University of Queensland. Quite a commute from the northern suburbs of Brisbane where I'm boarding.'

That would be those northern suburbs, one of which is Hendra.

'I know what you're thinking,' George Grave said to me. 'How does a bush brumby like me raise two beautiful talented daughters?'

That was not what I was thinking: more like, are a mob of crazed blowflies running amok in George's top paddock?

'Are they twins?' I said.

'Would you like them to be twins?'

That question could not possibly have a correct answer.

'We're twins,' Francine and Isobel answered together.

Dad was not done with me, yet. 'I would hate to be the man who wronged either of my daughters. By the way, Mr Funnyman, have you heard the one about the banker's daughters?'

I hadn't but I did hear the farmer's daughters cough in unison. 'No, I haven't,' I said.

'This destitute beef cattle farmer visits the big city and goes to a banker's house. The banker, who has two beautiful daughters, invites him in and breaks open a bottle of single malt whiskey for the destitute beef farmer and him. You with me so far, Mr Joker from the Big Smoke.'

Francine's voice was nervous beyond what you might expect of a daughter enduring an embarrassing parent. 'Dad, please,' she said.

Her sister Isobel chimed in. 'Dad, you're terrible at telling stories. Leave Steele alone.'

This just made George mad. 'I am not allowed to tell one lousy story in my own home. You think that too, Mr Hill.?'

'It's awlright by me, George. Is this one of those guess-what-really-happened riddles? Like the bloke hangs himself on a block of ice, sort of thing,' I said.

'Why would any bloke hang himself on a block of ice,' he said. He bored straight into my eyes. 'Out here, we use a tree.'

'If you can find one,' I said.

'I'm sure I could find one.' He swatted away a thought with a back hand sweep. 'Wouldn't waste it on suicide.' He looked directly into my eyes. 'A lynching's another matter,' he said.

I glanced nervously across at Isobel, serenely placing in her mouth a forkful of mashed potato, wrapped in gravy. I guess she was used to dining with a certifiable madman.

George was warming to his subject. 'They hung Westley Allan Dodd this year. First one in 28 years, they tell me. He asked for it.'

I was keen not to ask for it inadvertently. 'What did he do?''

'Don't you read the paper, Mr Funnypages?'

I do not read much beyond the racing form guide and on occasion the arts and entertainment section but surely I would have heard of a lynching in Birdsville. Maybe the locals kept it to themselves.

'Dodd was an American murderer, rapist and child molester,' George said.

Sounded all round, not a nice man. 'So that's what you meant by he asked for it,' I said.

George raised his eyes and shook his head. 'My words are not good enough and you gotta put some others in my mouth, Mr Funnylines. They asked Dodd how he would like to die and he said by hanging.'

'That showed some guts,' I said. 'I would have said old age.'

George curled the side of his lip in a snarl but all he said was, 'Hnnh.'

We ate in silence for a while until George said, 'He asked for his hanging to be televised live.'

'Dodd did?'

'You're catching up fast now, Mr City Slicker.'

'And was it?'

'Course not. That animal Dodd, all he wanted was fame. The clear-thinking executioners wanted him dead without a fuss.'

'I can see that,' I said.

George Grave stared unblinking to my eyes. 'Would people fuss over you, Mr Funnypot?'

I had lost my appetite. I ignored the question and nodded at my unfinished meal. The girls began to clear the plates. They brought apple pie and ice-cream.

'How come you had so much food prepared for dinner, George?" I asked.

'For tea,' he said. 'On account of the other young bloke.' He put his knuckles under his chin and stared ahead.

'We had another visitor,' Isobel said. She speaks too. 'Once.'

I may have looked uneasy. I felt it.

Francine touched me lightly on the shoulder and looked at her sister. 'Don't sound so dramatic, Issy. Another young man broke down last year and we had hardly any food in the place. It was embarrassing.'

George snapped out of his reverie. 'Embarrassing,' he agreed. 'For all we knew, it could have been his last meal.'

I coughed. A piece of pie must have gone down the wrong way. 'You a cattle farmer, Mr Grave?' I asked.

'Used to be, just like the one who visited the banker and his two daughters.' he said. 'That was before the wife passed on.'

I heard the girls tittering again and looked to see they were trying to hide smiles. Maybe George wasn't the only Grave of concern.

'I'm sorry,' I said.

'She passed on to Alice Springs and from there down to Adelaide. Ran away with my best mate.'

'You must miss him.'

'Miss who?'

'Your best mate.'

'Didn't I just get through telling you he ran away with my wife? Why would I miss him?'

'I'm sorry,' I said again, rather than tell him I was recycling a venerable old joke.

'He was a bank manager,' George said. 'They went to the Birdsville races together and never came back.'

I looked at him, trying to decipher whether he was making it up as he went along. There were far too many coincidences between my trip to Birdsville and his sorry tale, not to mention his unfinished joke about another banker and his daughters

'Is your mate the banker in your story?'

'Could be.' He pushed away his empty dessert plate. 'Getting late, time for me to take in the blanket show.' The blanket show is bedtime. The expression is so old it probably referred to the last show listened to on radio rather than watched on television

'What time is it?' I asked.

He looked at his watch. 'Six-thirty.'

'But you didn't finish your banker's daughters' story.'

'It'll keep. Besides, you won't like the ending. Hope you get to the races, tomorrow.'

George Grave ambled down the hall but turned after taking his hand from a door knob. 'The last young bloke did not make it.' He entered his bedroom.

Isobel removed the plates and Francine boiled the jug for coffee. 'Where would you like to sleep, Steele,' Francine asked.

Hendra, I thought. 'Anywhere,' I answered.

'You have a choice,' Isobel said. 'My room or Francine's.'

'What about the couch?'

'If you like,' Francine said. 'Or you might prefer the guest room.'

This whole family gave me the creeps with their unfathomable way with words. 'Is it true about your mother running away with your dad's best mate?'

'It's hardly a thing you'd make up.' Francine said.

'And he was a banker?'

'Yes,' Isobel said.

'And you two are twins?'

'You're on a roll,' Isobel said, speaking out of turn. 'We should go to the races with you, tomorrow.'

'That's if I get there.'

'You'll get there. Dad's got lengths of every thickness of radiator hose you can imagine in the four-wheel-drive,' Francine said.

'And heaps of water. He could have had you on your way to Birdsville within minutes, this evening, if he wanted to,' Isobel said.

'Why didn't he?'

Francine looked across at her twin who nodded. 'He likes you,' Francine said.

He likes me.

Isobel pranced across the room to flick the hair above my temple. 'A light plane spotted you hours ago and radioed Dad.'

'We could have picked you up ages ago,' Francine said.

'But Dad said you were probably a city slicker who needed a lesson,' Isobel said.

Francine had moved to the other side of my face. 'A lesson best taught by the boiling sun,' she said.

Something else made sense, now. 'So that's how you knew to prepare extra dinner?'

'You are gullible, Steele. You really believed that story about the other man,' Isobel said.

'Of course not,' I protested. 'I was just being polite.'

'We didn't feed him,' Francine said.

'Dad didn't like him,' Isobel said.

'He likes you.' Francine said.

I was George Grave's new best mate, bound for the Birdsville races. 'Your father said he'd never been to the horse races. But that's where your mother ran away with the banker.'

Between them they explained. George never had any inclination to go to the races. But his wife wanted to go, seeing they lived so close, only 85km away. George asks his best mate. You know how it goes: take my wife. His best mate does.

I was curious whether George tracked them down but didn't ask.

'Don't ask,' Isobel said.

'What?'

'You were going to ask whether we are virgins because we have lived in the Outback so long,' Francine said.

'But don't,' Isobel said.

'Don't ask,' Francine said.

'Let's play Trivial Pursuit,' Isobel said.

We did, for hours. They were more trivial than I or better at pursuit because I never won a game. They should put more horse-racing and rock-music questions in that board game. The twins ignored all my questions about whether their father tracked down his wife.

I did take the guest room. It was a long time before I found sleep. I kept dreading a knock at the door, no matter whose hand it belonged to.

I awoke one time to see dull light creeping around the edges of the window blind. I rose and put a pair of shorts over my boxers. I donned a Grateful-Dead T-shirt I had bought for a dollar at a charity shop. I blundered into the kitchen.

George sat at the table with a bath towel, a hand towel and a cake of soap in front of him. He wasn't drinking or eating or talking to anyone — just staring into space. He sighed. Without looking at me, he handed me the towels and soap.

'Don't waste the water; costs a fortune for the tanker to bring it in. The ute's fixed. Good car the EH but only a fool would drive a 30-year old one from Brisbane to Birdsville.'

'From Toowoomba and they're all 30-years old.'

He turned his face to hold his eyes on mine.

'Yours'll see 31. Were you hoping to see 30?'

'Hadn't made any plans but I guess I had dormant expectations.'

'Everyone has expectations. Orange juice, cereal, bacon and eggs, with toast is that awlright for breakfast?'

I could smell the bacon grilling. 'Last meal?'

'Country hospitality. I'll put it out on the eastern veranda.'

I found the eastern veranda after I showered. A smaller ironbark table held a glass of orange juice, a pot of coffee, pitcher of milk and hot buttered toast. I lifted an aluminium cover to reveal a plate of bacon, eggs, grilled tomato and fried mushrooms. Beside the 'shrooms was a note, written in a strong hand. 'Alice said not to eat the mushrooms.'

I finished the juice and was enjoying the filter coffee and toast when a soft pair of hands began massaging the back of my neck. I turned around. She was wearing blue pyjamas with white rabbits on them. Kind of cute, I suppose.

'Isobel, that's nice.'

'I'm Francine.'

`Fifty-fifty chance and I am wrong. You girls don't really want to go to the races with me.'

'I am Isobel. I thought you might have backed your judgement a bit longer, Steele.'

'I'm no good at games.'

'We'll see.'

I looked out over the veranda and I did see. Nothing. A couple of big dams, both shy on water, four paddocks, two barns, hale bales, even a bravely battling vegie garden. Not one cow.

'How many hectares out here, Isobel?'

'Dad talks in acres, 44 thousand. That's the family farm.'

'But you're not farming anything, Isobel,'

'Oh, I see. We should farm something, have a negative annual income and owe the bank more money. Why didn't Dad think of that? It takes a bright city boy to come up with such a master plan.'

'Toowoomba is only technically a city,' I said in my defence.

'Word to the wise, city boy. I wouldn't go sticking with that Toowoomba story. Could be dangerous.'

'I'm not going to make it to the Birdsville races, am I, Isobel?'

'Why ever not? Such suspicion in a man not yet 30.'

'Are you and Francine really twins?'

'You're obsessed with that and we answered you last night. Maybe Dad's right: you might be stupid. I don't know what he sees in you.'

'Are you the twins in George's story?'

'You are getting nowhere with these questions, Steele, though I am answering truthfully. Maybe you need to think laterally, like the person on the ice block. More coffee?'

'You're playing with me.'

'Perhaps. Did you bring a lot of money for the races?'

'I don't have a lot of money, period.'

'Pity. It'll have to be for sport.'

'Did your dad kill your mother and her lover?'

`You'd have to ask him.'

'Is the bank about to foreclose on the property?'

'No.'

I stood up. 'I am going to ask your dad to finish his story.'

'No, don't do that. We are still playing.'

'Game over,' I said. 'Where's Francine?'

'You wanna play with me?' Francine said from down the hall. She wore a two-piece white nightie, revealing until she tied a light dressing gown over it.

Isobel was annoyed. 'Steele wants to know how the story ends when dad visited his brother in Sydney.'

'His brother? His brother's a banker, too?

'Investment banker. Dad says they're the worst kind but he and his brother were always close?

'Were?' I said.

'Are. Are close,' Francine said. Down in Sydney, they just had a few drinks. Dad gave his nieces presents and stayed a while. Hardly earth-shattering.'

'His nieces are twins and his brother's a banker,' I said.

'Having twins runs in the Grave family,' Isobel said.

'And your mother?'

'She writes to us all the time,' Francine said. 'Phones when we are away studying. Dad pretends he doesn't know a thing about it.'

'The farm makes money doing nothing?'

'Dad writes comedy scripts for film and television. He even writes bits and pieces for US TV. His income fluctuates but in the end it pays well enough to send us to uni and prevent him from flogging a dead horse, um, cow,' one of them said.

'He doesn't write comedy scripts. That can't be true,' I said

'Please yourself,' Isobel said. 'I bet he's been taking notes since after dinner which, by the way, he does not call tea. That was for your benefit. And he doesn't ever go to bed at six-thirty.'

'And when you say he likes me?'

'As a character,' Isobel said. 'He says he wants to use you.'

'And all that ominous flirting you pair were doing with me?'

'What can we say?' Isobel said.

'Like father like daughter,' they said in unison.

The girls decided to give the races a miss which was a bit of a shame as I found them attractive, now I was fairly certain they were not planning to kill me.

George insisted he fill the ute's tank from his petrol supplies. He said it was to make up for all the staring he had done to watch my reaction.

He disguised advice as an observation 'They tell me most of the 6000 visitors to the Birdsville races fly in.'

'Flying to Birdsville sounds good,' I said. 'Next time I'll take a different route.'

'Which one?' George said.

'Probably Natalie. She stood by me during the money drought.'

George said I was a stupid clown. The family waved me on my way.

Hi Lily Hi Lily Hi Lo
R. William Penshorn

I wandered along a lonely beach.
I saw a fair maiden well within reach.

Upon the sand dunes stood an old empty dwelling.
What lay in store for me, there was no telling.

I was lured inside where the maid had her way.
I'd only just met her but there we did lay.

The passion we shared was out of this world.
My hair stood on end. My toes tingled and curled.

I'd never known anything like it before.
I felt she would be in my heart evermore.

Was this old shack 'neath the blue sky above
The place where I'd found eternal true love?

I could not believe what next she did say.
The words that she spoke were 'It's now time to pay.'

Shocked and bewildered, I kissed her lips twice.
She changed in an instant and became cold as ice.

I went to the door of that deserted old shack.
Rushed to the beach and ran all the way back.

So realistic and true her existence did seem.
But I awoke to find out it had all been a dream.

HOPE AMID WAR

Paimarire Teague

JAGER Robinson awoke to the sound of screaming. A sound so rare in Oxford that the young boy immediately dismissed it for the cry of a bird, at least until his father ran in and threw him over his shoulder.

'Dad?' Jager groaned, sleepily.

'Shh! Jager you must be silent,' his father whispered, running towards the kitchen.

'But daddy what's wrong?'

'Nothing, son, nothing at all, we're just going to play hide and seek, okay?' his dad said putting him into the dumbwaiter. 'No matter what you hear, you must not make a noise, okay Jager.'

Jager nodded, his curly hair falling across his eyes.

'Okay, daddy,' he whispered, placing his chubby index finger to his lips. 'Me be quiet.'

'Yes, good boy, Jager, you be quiet,' his dad said, leaning in and placing a firm kiss on his son's head. 'I love you Jager, okay? You and your mum mean the world to me.'

'Me love daddy, too!' Jager shouted throwing his hands into the air and grinning wildly.

Tears formed in the eyes of Jager's dad.

'Hush now son you must be quiet, okay, no more noise,' he whispered.

Jager nodded, not saying a word.

'I love you Jager, remember that.'

Jager nodded again as his father leant in and kissed him for what would surely be the last time.

As his father pulled back, he placed his finger to his lips and pulled the lever to lower the dumbwaiter to basement level.

The sight that young Jager later beheld was one that no eight-year old should ever have to witness. After hours sitting cooped up in the dumbwaiter, with his hands to his ears trying to block out the horrible shrieking that seemed to come from every direction, the small child let himself out, crawling up the basement stairs and standing on tiptoes to reach the handle.

Once the door was open, Jager stood staring at formerly pristine white walls streaked red with gore and blood.

13 years later

CAPTAIN Jager Robinson sat with Major Jones, General Matthews, and five other army officials discussing the topic of massacres that had been wreaking havoc across the whole of London since 2195, 13 years ago. A very morbid conversation to start the day with.

'These southerners have gone too far this time!' General Matthews said, indicating a picture on the projecting board behind them.

The image was one with bodies littering the streets of Northampton, or rather the limbs of bodies. This particular street ran red with blood.

Captain Jager stared ahead refusing to look at the image that hit so close to home. He looked across the table at his uncle Major Jones. They were relatives by all but blood, and Jager would be forever grateful to the ageing warrior who had turned a scared eight-year-old boy into the man he was now.

Major Jones leaned into General Matthews and whispered to him.

Jager received a small glance before the image on the screen vanished. Jager released a breath he didn't know he was holding and stared at the blank screen.

Major Jones could not help but feel a pang of sadness. The poor boy before him was so young and yet he had witnessed almost as much violence as the General himself. 'Captain Jager, what are your opinions on how to stop these bloodbaths caused by the southern scum?'

'I hope you don't mind me asking, but how do we know it's the Southerners doing this?' Jager inquired watching as the General's eyebrows rose.

'Are you implying that it is someone else launching these attacks, Captain?' the general questioned.

Jager nodded. 'Yes sir, you see, during my time as corporal, the attacks launched by the Southerners were ones of less violence and also none of the weapons in the whole of England is able to remove the limbs from human bodies with such damage. For example, all the weapons which we use nowadays involve lasers, which merely burn holes through the victim They are incapable of splintering the bones of the human body the way the victims we have found, have had done to them.'

Jager paused to draw a breath. 'However the only weapons I can think of to cause so much damage are found in the museums that the army has neglected to burn to the ground. The people of the past called them axes.'

'And you believe these axes are being used in the massacres we have been witnessing for the past 13 years, am I right, Captain?'

'Yes, General and I also have reason to believe that the southern townsfolk have no role in this, because all the museums in that area were burned to the ground by our men to create strongholds for our weapons. The only museums that remain are the ones here in Northampton and the ones in the East where there is supposedly only barren wastelands. If we were to take a close look as to where these massacres first started it would lead you towards the east.'

Jager walked towards a map that hung on a wall. Red pins showed a distinct path leading from the East. Jager followed the trail with his finger and let a small, barely imperceptible gasp leave his lips. 'They're coming,' he whispered.

'What do you mean they're coming, Captain? Who's coming?' the General asked

'They are,' Jager shouted, bringing up the image of all the dead bodies in Northampton, '*They* are coming, the murderers; the bastards of the dead are coming.' Jager had said it even louder.

General Matthews nudged the young Captain to the side gently. 'Well I'll be damned,' he muttered turning towards the Major. 'I think it's time we told the boy.'

If Jager didn't know better he could have sworn he saw traces of tears in his uncle's eyes.

The Major nodded. 'Yes,' he said. 'I think it's time.'

10 minutes later
'NO, I don't believe it!' Jager said stubbornly. 'It's not possible.'

'It is Captain and you have to believe it. You don't have a choice. I didn't think it was possible but it seems the reasons for these massacres are the army's fault.'

'I cannot believe it. You cannot just create super-enhanced beings. You *can't!*'

'You can and we did,' the General said.

'Oh, and pigs can fly and chickens have teeth,' Jager mocked

'Captain Jager, you were given your position because of your skills and logic, so do not laugh at such a thing,' General Matthews snapped.

'Exactly, I was chosen for my *logic!* And nothing about *this* is logical. You are basically telling me that my father was murdered by supernatural beings along with the whole of Northampton and Oxford.'

'Jager, the General is telling the truth,' Major Jones whispered. 'I was good friends with your father and we were both part of the team that created these beings. But they were not meant to be violent. In fact they were not even meant to move. When they were created they did nothing. They didn't talk. They didn't move. They didn't blink. They had no minds of their own and they didn't listen to a word we said. That's why we sent them to the Eastern Wastelands, because they could cause no trouble there, and eventually they would have just starved themselves to death.'

Jager looked at the man who had raised him for 13 years with barely concealed disgust. 'You wanted them to just starve themselves?' He frowned deeply. 'We are the army, we're meant to protect people not leave them to die.'

'You could barely consider them people, Jager,' The General said.

'And whose fault was that?' Jager barked. 'You mixed their DNA with something you didn't know the name of or what it contained. You made normal humans beings brain-dead zombies. Then you cast them away to die in the Eastern lands, and, because of your stupid dreams of a super army, thousands of people have lost their lives.

'You turned normal people into revenge-crazed monsters. Kudos to you General.' Jager glowered at the man who was in charge of him.

'Jager, stop glaring at the General. I'm as much to blame a he is,' Major Jones stated.

'Oh don't worry, Major, I blame you too.' Jager gave a sigh of defeat. 'I also blame my dad. Why couldn't you all just be content with what you had? That way none of us would be here.'

'We are both gravely sorry, Jager, even though we both know our apologies won't change a thing.'

'It's okay; there is no point in dwelling on the past when we have a far worse future to overcome,' Jager whispered and gave a small grin. 'Now if you are both willing to listen I think I might have quite a good plan.'

48 hours later

THE darkness was absolute. At every turn nothing could be seen, nothing except the faint flickering light that emitted from a small house in the middle of the town. Its dim light was a glowing beacon to any eyes that cared to wander the streets at that time of night.

The darkness was broken as the glint of sharp blades fragmented the darkness like shards of a broken mirror. The low wail of a baby made its way through the brick walls of the house into the open air of the streets. The brief noise was followed by a tense silence, shattered as the sound of a thousand shrieking birds filled the air. Quick shadows darted through the darkness towards the house like a swarm of black angry wasps.

Inside the house Jager felt his blood run cold as he peered through the window shutters. He snarled into his communicator. 'General! This is Jager, the targets are moving towards the Beacon. From the shadows I count at least fifty and that's only at the front of the house. How many of these freaking monstrosities did you create?'

'I'd prefer not to tell you son, but it's probably best if I did. From what you said there are at least another forty.'

Jager groaned.

'I want you out of the house now, Jager. I have three-hundred men with me, ready for the signal. I would prefer to have you with us. I already have too much of your family's blood on my hands. I don't need anymore, so get your hide down here, now the back gate is secured.'

'Don't worry. I don't plan on dying in this hole, not alone anyway.'

'That's my boy. Now hurry'

'I'm already on my way.'

Jager ran down a flight of stairs and out through the back door of the house. He ran across the lawn, his gun at the ready. Ahead he saw two guards at the gate straining their eyes against the impeding darkness.

Jager ran towards them at top speed when suddenly one of the guards was lifted off his feet. Dark fingers forced their way through the guard's pale throat. The soldier's blood spilt down his neck.

The other guard turned too late as his partner was flung across the yard by the predator. Jager shouted a warning to the guard and aimed his gun at the dark figure. A laser shot from the gun. The figure crumpled and the guard who was closer to it continued to shoot laser after laser into the aberration before him.

Jager ran up to the guard who had been flung across the yard and felt tears spring in his eyes.

'A *child*,' he whispered. 'He was but a child'

'Don't cry for me, Captain,' came a weak voice. 'I will have died for an honourable cause.'

'You're so young,' Jager said.

'You aren't much older than me, Captain. Just do me a favour and make sure every one of those bastards don't live to see another day. They killed my family and deserve to die,' he muttered, before drawing his last breath.

Jager closed the boy's eyes before standing up.

'They killed mine; too. I'm just glad you don't know who created them.'

'Captain?' the second guard asked, confused by his superior's words.

'Never mind soldier, quick let us hurry towards the others.'

The soldier nodded and Jager stooped to pick up the dead guard's body.

'What are you doing, Captain?' the soldier asked.

'If any of us survive this I want this boy treated to a proper burial. I refuse to leave him here to be torn to pieces by our enemies.'

The soldier moved towards Jager and lifted his dead partner from his arms.

'At the moment Captain, you are our number-one priority. The General needs you in the front lines with him, I will take care of little Johnny.' The older guard looked at the young man in his arms.

Breaking with tradition, Jager saluted the man before him. He nodded and let the older man with the young corpse in his arms go before him.

After a few moments of running the two men made their way to the arranged location that would be their temporary headquarters.

By the time they arrived, they realised that the army were already engaged in the battle and several of their men were on the ground.

Major Jones forced his way through the ever increasing crowd that was beginning to encircle Jager and grabbed the boy roughly by the wrist.

'Quickly, Jager, the General is worried sick about you. He was about to get everyone to abort the mission if you didn't show up. It seems you are his rock in this mission, my boy.'

'Wait Major, there is a young man back there. I believe his name is Johnny. He died only minutes ago. If anybody survives this mission I want them to give him a proper burial. He was only young.'

Jones nodded. 'Then it shall be done, boy, but you must hurry.'

He pulled Jager through the crowd, towards a long line of men fully armed and dressed in black and silver protective gear. 'General I found him,' Major Jones said.

'Good bring him up here.' Even as the General said the words, Jager made his way to the front line.

'Good to see you, Captain, good to see you,' the General said.

'You too, General.' Jager turned his steely blue eyes to face the shadows.

'You ready for this boy?' the General asked

'I've learnt that I don't really have a choice as to whether I'm ready or not, General. We are the army. No matter what, we have to be ready.'

'Damn right boy, now let's give these scum a taste of their own medicine.'

Though feeling a little foolish, Jager raised his fist into the night sky and shouted, 'ONWARDS! FOR ENGLAND!'

The blood and gore of the dead and wounded had painted a tableau of horror across the land. The blood seeped so deeply into the ground that Jager feared the earth beneath his feet would be that one colour for the rest of eternity. The bodies of his enemies and fellow soldiers were strewn like fleshy mounds of dirt and rocks.

Of the four hundred men who had played their part in this tragic war, only fifty had survived. All the abominations that had killed his father and the whole of Northampton were dead.

Among the dead lay the General and Jager's Uncle, Major Jones. Although Jager longed to grieve over the bodies of such honourable men, he decided that would have to wait for later. Now, he was the highest ranking officer and needed to help the injured to safety.

Jager sighed. *So many dead,* he thought, *and for what? Greed? Power? Such pointless wars disgust me when everything could have been prevented if everybody would just be content with what they have.*

As the sun rose on the dreadful scene beneath it, the people of England rejoiced in their sudden peace. Many brave warriors, who had worked so hard to earn that small piece of tranquillity, lay in deep graves or begged the gods for a reason why they too did not perish with the rest.

A STEP TOO FAR

Anne Olsson

IT is a sorry tale. It tells of the fruits of ambition that withered in the sun, and fell unwanted to the ground, to rot away unseen and unappreciated. So it is, for ambition without knowledge and discernment is a futile goal.

Raz we called him. He disliked being called Roger. He was always the most confident of us five, handsome, clever and self-assured. He was ambitious and seemed destined for great things. How could we know, in the last days of our schooling, that life would play such tricks upon us? We were young, naive and inexperienced, and it seemed that the world was at our feet.

It was 1968. Our school days had come to an end. We were gathered at the beach at Arrawarra, bravely drinking beer around a camp fire, celebrating our freedom from study and regimentation. The moon was full, and the night air was cool and clear. The moonlight and the light of the camp fire reflected in the waves as they swept up onto the sand and fell away into the blackness of the ocean. We were watching the flames as they were teased by the wind. Raz stood up and placed another piece of wood onto the blaze.

'Well, no more school for us!' he exclaimed.

Colin, playful and impudent Colin, raised the can in his hand jubilantly. 'No more boring economics! No more grumpy teachers!'

Raz reached over and playfully tousled his hair, but Colin pulled away in mock dismay. 'That's all very well for you, Col,' Raz exclaimed. 'You'll be working with your dad soon and earning decent money. Liz and I'll be slaving away at university in a few months.'

'You needn't boast. We weren't all as smart as you.'

'You're smart enough, Col. You were just too lazy to study,' Raz laughed. 'Going to school doesn't make you a student any more than swinging from a tree makes you a monkey.'

I watched Raz as he looked across the flames at Daniel who was unobtrusively poking the fire with a stick, his face expressionless.

Daniel seemed to be in a world of his own. He was always uncommunicative and a little strange, but Raz was usually able to break through his shell and reach him. Daniel's vulnerability was perceptible. The look Raz gave him now was almost tender.

'You'll be okay next year, Dan,' he said quietly. 'You'll enjoy college. You'll be doing what you love best.' Without speaking, Daniel raised his eyes and met Raz's gaze briefly, then returned to stoking the coals.

Stephen, lanky, carefree Stephen, drained the last of the beer from his can and tossed it onto the sand behind him. 'Remember what Mr. Brazen used to say to you, Col? - *I'd advise you to keep your mouth shut and let others think you an imbecile, than to open it and remove all doubt.* He never was very original, but he was always smug and sarcastic when he spoke to you.'

Colin laughed. 'The brazen liar! He had no sense of humour, that was his problem.'

'Mrs. Cosgrove had a great sense of fun,' I remarked. 'She was a lousy history teacher but she did have a sense of humour. She told me that to pilfer ideas from one book was plagiarism, but to rob from many books was research.' I chuckled. 'I put that advice to good use.' I was the only female amongst us. These boys were my mates, not the local girls I judged as mindless and effeminate.

The banter continued but Daniel spoke not a word. He stood up unobtrusively, and walked barefoot away from the fire down to the water's edge. Raz followed him with his gaze until he suddenly cried out, kicked off his thongs and ran after him. Raz grabbed Daniel's hands and pulled him into the waves.

'Come on, you lot,' he called to us, 'get your gear off and come for a swim. Let's wash away the grime of school.'

Daniel was laughing, protesting about the coldness of the water.

Perhaps we were all a little crazy that night, perhaps the beer had weakened our inhibitions, but one by one we shed our clothes and ran over the wet sand into the cold waters of the ocean. It was madness but we did not stop laughing. We finally returned to the warmth of the fire, Raz and Daniel in sodden clothes. Raz joked that this was our christening, our initiation into the world beyond school. The bonds of our friendship were strong that night, and we vowed to stay closely connected in the years ahead, no matter where our lives would lead us.

We did meet regularly in those early years – several times in Coffs Harbour, twice in Sydney, and once we holidayed together at Noosa. Raz completed his degree and was working for a Sydney legal firm. Colin was working in his father's plumbing business. I was teaching in Tamworth and Stephen was a bank teller in Grafton. Daniel surprised us by finding a well-paying job with a company in Brisbane that manufactured hearing aids. Life seemed to be prospering for all of us.

The cracks started to appear in the structure of our lives when we moved into our thirties. Daniel was still working for the same company, but Colin had had a major argument with his father and moved to Casino to build a business of his own. I was still teaching but felt my life was stagnating. Raz and Stephen had both married, Stephen to a troubled girl he had known at school and Raz to a beautiful blonde he had met in Sydney. There were already rumours that the blonde was having an affair with one of Raz's clients, but we judged them as idle talk. Only Daniel seemed content with his life.

We were meeting less frequently, perhaps once or twice a year. Occasionally one of us would miss the gathering. Colin's business was not successful, and Stephen was struggling to cope with his wife's mental-health problems. We began to see the first signs of Raz's gambling addiction. He had come north for a break from work that weekend. His wife had just left him and he was struggling with depression. I had suggested we meet up in Coffs Harbour, hoping that the rest of us could offer him some support and guidance.

Colin got a lift down from Casino, and I drove across from Nana Glen where I was now teaching. Only Daniel was not with us. Raz's face was grey, his expression anxious, when four of us went out to the local RSL club that Saturday evening. During our meal the conversation was desultory. After we had eaten, Raz left us and found distraction at a poker machine. We saw little of him for the rest of the night. When we met up again the following day, he appeared agitated and restless. He seemed to find little pleasure in our company, and was anxious to return to Sydney.

The dark shadow that hung over Raz's life lingered for several months. When he met a gentle English woman and reported that he was in love again, I was concerned that insufficient time had passed for the wounds of his divorce to heal. However this new relationship prospered, and the rest of us rejoiced that his life was on track again. When we finally got to meet her, we liked her. Sharon was not beautiful, nor was she well educated, but she was warm-hearted, sincere and funny. There was an honesty and openness described on her face that drew me to her. With her at his side, Raz regained his old confidence and zest for living.

They were married during the summer in the old Anglican church in Lane Cove. They were both happy and excited. When the five of us gathered together at the wedding, it was as though we were at school again, playful, teasing and irreverent. The laughter and affection we shared was palpable.

Together Raz and Sharon bought an imposing house in Manly. Raz would catch the ferry across the harbour to reach the legal firm he had joined. When I heard that Sharon was pregnant with their first child, I believed that Raz's problems were finally behind him. His son was born on a wet and windy day at the end of June.

Two years later, after the birth of their second child, I flew to Sydney to visit them and meet the little girl who was to be my God-daughter. She was a bonny girl but Sharon was struggling with post-natal depression. Raz however appeared happy and contented. When I watched him holding his daughter in his arms so proudly, I felt glad of heart. I heard him whisper to her, 'Always be true to yourself, little one. Never deny who you are because someone might have a problem with it. Never give up your dreams to please anyone.' Why did those words sound so poignant to me?

I had to return to work soon after the christening but I kept in contact regularly. As the months passed, I began to sense that Raz was not being completely open with me. I heard an edge to his voice and he seemed reluctant to tell me the simplest details of his life.

Several years later they moved to Brisbane. The grand house in Sydney was sold and they bought a small house in Boondall. Raz was reticent about the reasons for the move but I could see that Sharon was very unhappy.

He found a position with a legal firm in Brisbane city but seemed restless and ill at ease. When I questioned him about this, he laughed nervously and proclaimed he needed to get away from the hypocritical crowd in Sydney. I did not believe him. I was thankful that he and Daniel were spending time together now. It seemed impossible that he would lie to Daniel.

Our high school held a reunion in August that year. It was the gathering of the clan again, the five of us once more together. The bonds between us were still strong, and we had a gay time with our old schoolmates. There were festivities at the school and a formal dinner on the Saturday evening. The memories came streaming back as we looked at old photographs and explored the classrooms that had been so familiar to us. At the dinner I noticed that Raz was drinking heavily. It did not concern me at the time, because after all, were we not celebrating? We continued partying at a hotel afterwards, and Raz's behaviour was becoming embarrassing. We took him back to his motel room, but he resisted us all the way. It dampened our spirits. When we met up again the next day, Raz appeared to be his old self again and we thought no more of it.

I did not see Raz again for more than a year, but Daniel told me about the good work that Raz was doing. He was writing a book on the resolution of backyard disputes, and had been providing a free legal service in Aspley for people on low incomes. My optimism was undermined when Colin came to visit me. He had spent the previous weekend with Raz and Sharon, and reported that Raz was gambling again and drinking excessively.

'Sharon is not happy,' he revealed. 'She says she's had enough. She says the children are frightened of him when he's been drinking, and there is no money for their basic necessities.' He ran his fingers through his greying hair and looked up at me with consternation. 'I think she's planning to leave him'.

Three weeks from that day I heard that she had left and taken the children. Raz was distraught, and so began the troubled days of arguments and legalities that led to their divorce eighteen months later. The dark days that followed saw Raz sinking deep into self-pity and helplessness. I drove up to Brisbane to visit him, but found him unreachable. The drinking continued unabated. He lost his job but he still found money somewhere to meet his thirst for alcohol.

On a visit to Brisbane several years later, I arranged to meet Daniel. He took me to visit Raz who was in a ward in the Redcliffe hospital. He was now suffering from diabetes. He lay quietly in the hospital bed, his skin sallow and grey, yet a smile lit up his face when he saw me. I was glad I had come. For a moment I saw a glimpse of the Raz of old, cheerful, playful and kind. It was to be the last time I saw him.

Two years later I was in Brisbane again and arranged to have lunch with Daniel. He was still in contact with Raz, and visited him regularly. When I asked him how Raz was faring, he was non-committal.

'Do his children visit him?' I asked. He shook his head.

'He meant a lot to us, didn't he?' I said.

'He still means a lot to me,' he replied defensively. 'He has always been my best friend.' He eyed me warily. 'I may forget what someone has said to me, or I may forget what they did, but I will never forget how they made me feel.'

So I left him that day very solemnly, thinking about the five of us and where our lives had led us. What did it all mean? I did not know.

The funeral procession wound slowly up the hill, until, one by one, the cars entered the cemetery gates and came to rest in the car park. An elderly gentleman was laying fresh flowers on a nearby gravestone and turned to watch us solemnly as we stepped out of the cars. All the mourners walked across the lawn to the grave site and gathered around the open pit.

I stood back from the main group, watching the faces of those who had come to see the body of this man, my friend of old, being laid in its final resting place. Neither of his children or his ex-wives were among the mourners. My eyes were damp with unshed tears. Colin and Stephen were standing at the edge of the grave, looking solemn and dismal. Daniel held himself erect beside me, stricken with grief. The anguish in his face disturbed me. I reached out and gently hooked my fingers through his. He showed no reaction but did not pull away. So I stood there, quietly holding his hand, and let the tears roll down my cheeks unhindered.

I could not understand why this was happening. I felt bewildered. This man had meant so much to us. He had been our champion. He had been the strong one, the clever one, the one who showed the greatest promise. Why had he died so ungraciously, in poverty in a dirty hovel, without kith or kin beside him? Why?

The words the priest spoke did not penetrate through the confused thoughts that clouded my mind. What meaning could they have held for me anyway? The priest had not known the man I had known. As I watched the coffin being lowered into the earth, I felt Daniel's hand tighten in mine. As clods of earth were tossed onto the coffin, his attempt to maintain his composure was abandoned and he sobbed convulsively.

When the last words had been uttered and the mourners began dispersing, the four of us walked slowly away together. I was still struggling with disbelief and confusion.

'How did this happen?' I cried. 'How could he have died without anyone knowing? Without anyone at his side? And not to be found for three days! I don't understand it.'

'He'd been ill for a long time, Liz. You knew he was an alcoholic. His liver was destroyed.' Colin looked down at me uneasily as he spoke. 'He had been doing his best to kill himself with alcohol for years.'

Stephen sighed. 'I am darned if I can understand how he came to make such a mess of his life. He could've done anything, been anybody.'

Colin shrugged his shoulders. 'He married the wrong women, and he gambled away anything of any value that he had. His drinking lost him the last shreds of any respect his children may have had for him. You can't blame them for that.'

Daniel had been listening without speaking, but he stopped and faced us grimly. 'Who are you to speak of Raz like that?' he protested. 'You're supposed to be his friends, but you're so self-centred you couldn't see how amazing he was. You didn't know him. None of you. And where were you during these last years of his life when he needed you? He was a fine man. An exceptional man. You didn't know who he really was, how kind he was. He'd help anyone in need of a friend. He was the best person I ever knew. What right have you to judge him?' He spat out the words. 'Your judgement of Raz does not describe who he was. It describes who you are. He was better than all you lot put together.'

I was taken aback. It was the longest speech I had ever heard Daniel make. I knew how much he loved Raz, how much he was hurting now, but I had no answers for him. He had spent far more time with Raz in recent years than any of us. I could see that he understood Raz in a way we did not. And what he said was true. We had no right to judge. No, we had no right to judge.

He turned from us now and strode away angrily, his sobbing more controlled. I knew I could not let him leave us like this. I ran after him and thrust my arm through his. He made a half-hearted attempt to pull away, but I held my arm firm.

As we walked on, Colin and Stephen hurried up to us and draped an arm over each of our shoulders. In a brooding silence we walked together back to the car park. But I sensed another presence with us. I knew it was the last time that the five of us would be together as one, because Raz's spirit walked with us.

The Outback

Vera Murray

The scorching heat,
Burns feet and land,
Blistering paint,
On red tin roofs.

Pepperina trees,
Weep leaves and bark,
Clogging the drains,
On the dairy roofs.

Windmill blades barely move;
Giving little moisture,
To the parched and brittle,
Crack-patterned earth.

Dingoes and Crows,
Strip raw meat,
From carcasses,
Of dead kangaroos.

From his homestead,
The farmer squints,
Vainly scanning,
A cloud-free sky.

He prays for rain,
To ease the pain,
Of watching crops,
Degenerate.

With his herd scattered,
And near dry his wells,
The family all leave,
For town, to wait.

Their stay seems endless,
But, they don't allow,
Their faith to wane,
While waiting for the change.

When dark clouds appear,
And quickly join up,
The farmer, and his wife,
Watch them anxiously.

At last those pregnant clouds,
Heavy downpours release,
To give birth and new life,
To a brand new cycle.

Relieved, and joy full,
They return to their farm,
But now that they're back,
They face a flood.

ALPHA OMEGA MOMENTS

Ronald Holt

ANNIE Howard was a delightful, attractive young lady, full of life and enthusiasm. Her bubbly personality was infectious and her popularity with her peers knew no bounds. Due to both her academic and sporting achievements, success followed her in all her endeavours. She came from a reasonably well-off loving family in which her parents doted on her.

After finishing as Dux of her high school she studied at university and soon found employment in one of the largest stock broking firms, Burrows.

Annie was very popular with her male contemporaries but she never had a steady boyfriend, preferring to establish herself in her career first. Annie's life had always been wonderful and her future prospects bright. Some thought she had led a charmed existence but she recognised early that life was made up of special events which often determined the paths people would follow. She called these *Alpha Omega moments* where one's past, present and future directions intersected, shaping that person's destiny. To her it was a matter of opportunity recognising those moments and taking advantage of life's challenges.

Little did she realise as she sat on the train to work that morning deeply engrossed in her Kindle Tablet that her life was about to change. At one station a number of passengers boarded and found seating in the carriage where Annie sat. She did not take much notice until she glanced up to see how far the train still had to travel to the city. It was then that she saw him.

Their eyes met and she glanced away quickly. Annie sensed that somebody had been watching her and she did not know whether to feel flattered or embarrassed. He was tall, well built, obviously from regular gym sessions, and very good looking. He was dressed in smart business attire. His thick dark hair was neatly groomed. Everything about him gave the impression of a person of some substance in his profession, whatever that was.

Annie's eyes dropped back onto her tablet but she could no longer concentrate on the story which had previously held her spellbound. Her gaze drifted back towards him. When she saw him looking in her direction, she quickly looked down again.

There was something about him, something different from her usual male acquaintances. She did not believe in love at first sight that was for silly irrational school girls but there was some attraction she could not explain. He alighted from the train one station from the city and she watched him walk along the platform with another well-dressed young man as the train moved away. She packed her tablet knowing that she could no longer concentrate. In any event the next station was hers. She tried to put his image aside thinking that she might never see him again. That day went slowly and her thoughts constantly returned to him, wondering if he would be on the train the next day.

Disappointingly for Annie he was not. Disappointment was not something that Annie had much experience with. She tried to comfort herself with the thought that she had her work and that was her goal at this stage of her life. He had not been on the train before, or at least she had not seen him, and this may have been only a once-off trip for him. Nevertheless she still intended to look for him on the train each morning.

The next week he was back. Some days he was alone but on others he was sitting with the young man she had seen him with on the platform. She did not take much notice of the companion as she was becoming infatuated with what was becoming her 'dream man'. She tried exchanging smiles with him but nothing happened except that she still sensed that someone was watching her when she was reading. To find out more about him she tried to listen to the conversations between him and his friend. The name, Brian, was mentioned by the companion and although not certain if that was her dream man's name, she used it in her imagination as if it was.

Annie was starting to feel agitated that 'her dream man' was not taking any notice of her. It seemed to her that something special would have to happen to change the present situation. Her wish was met the day the train was delayed. Brian was not sitting in the carriage so she was disappointed but her focus was an important meeting called by her company's general manager. Something was going on at work and she needed to be there on time. As soon as the train stopped, she jumped out and headed for the exit. The heel on one of her best high-heel shoes broke and she crashed heavily onto the platform. Gingerly, she tried to get up when she felt a hand on her arm assisting her to her feet. She turned to see who the Good Samaritan was. It was him!

'Are you alright? That was quite a fall you just took,' he said in a sympathetic tone. 'My name is Brian. I have seen you regularly on the train.'

She felt embarrassed by her fall but replied, 'Thank you. I am alright. My name is Annie. Just when I was running late for a meeting, this happens. I will have to go barefoot and get my shoe fixed later. My father told me not to wear such high heels. Maybe I should have listened to him.'

'As long as you are not hurt that is all that matters,' Brian said sympathetically. 'I am running late too. I will have to hurry. Maybe I will see you on the train again.'

Despite being a bit sore and shaken, Annie was elated as she watched him hurry along the platform. *It was an Alpha Omega moment*, she thought. *Where the old life comes to an end, the Omega, and the new life begins, the Alpha.* She had to hurry to get to the meeting and her thoughts of Brian would have to wait.

Annie arrived late but just in time to hear her boss say, 'We are on the verge of losing one of our biggest clients – the Hopwood Group. We have had their account for many years and we will have to fight to keep them. I don't know what has happened but they are planning to take their business to our competitors, Carringtons. If we don't succeed we will have to reduce our staff numbers. I don't want to do that so I want everyone to try to find out what has happened and what we need to do to keep Hopwoods.'

The enormity of this announcement hit Annie hard. She was the last one to be employed here and would probably be the first to go if there were staff cuts. Her *Alpha Omega moment* with Brian might have to wait until her future was resolved.

She saw Brian regularly on the train for the next few days but apart from a smile or a nod of acknowledgement nothing further transpired except that she still had a sense of being watched. Brian was usually with his friend and Annie surmised that this is why he did not speak with her. Although her thoughts were on her work, she continued to relive his arm on hers as he helped her up from her fall. Nothing was happening at work to resolve the Hopwood situation and an air of depression was coming over her usual bubbly nature. Her parents noticed the change but she passed it off with being tired from the workload.

If things were not already causing concerns for Annie, the next day she saw Brian waiting on the station platform hand in hand with a gorgeous blond. Annie was close enough to see that she was wearing an engagement ring. Annie could not believe what a fool she had been to expect that Brian would not be in some relationship. The *Alpha Omega moment* she felt when she first spoke to Brian burst like a bubble.

She tried to involve herself in her Kindle but it was no good. She had a feeling that all the good times she had experienced in her life had evaporated.

'Hello, may I sit next to you,' she heard a male voice shyly enquire. She looked up and recognised that it was Brian's friend who was speaking to her.

'Of course,' Annie responded. She had never taken much notice of the friend as her attention was always so focused on Brian. He also was quite handsome and well dressed.

'My name is Bill. I have seen you regularly traveling on this train. I talked my friend, Brian, into sitting in this carriage so I could see you. I have always wanted to meet you but I have been reluctant to open any conversation in fear of looking like a fool. But today I decided to build up courage and talk to you. Brian is with his fiancée today so he does not want my company.'

Annie sat dumbfounded not knowing what to say. It struck her that the person she could sense watching her was Bill not Brian.

'I was wondering if you would like to have lunch with me sometime. I work in the city and we could meet where ever you choose. I am sorry but I don't even know your name.'

'It's Annie,' she finally responded. 'And I would like to have lunch with you.'

Her response then hit home with her. She had agreed to go to lunch with a perfect stranger, someone she had only seen a few times on the train. *Why did I do that*, she wondered. But then why not, she asked herself, nothing else is going right. Was this an *Alpha Omega moment*? There was one way to find out.

'How about lunch today? I am available if you are,' Bill suggested.

'Alright. I have nothing on at lunch time today. I work at Burrows and there is a nice restaurant in our building,' Annie suggested.

'That's interesting. My friend, Brian, works for your opposition, Carringtons,' Bill observed and then added, 'I know that restaurant. I have been there a few times with my father.'

'Where do you work, Bill?' Annie enquired becoming curious about Bill and his connection with Brian.

'I work at Hopwoods,' Bill responded. 'My name is Bill Hopwood and my father owns the company. My father told me I had to start at the bottom and work my way up with no special favours. Hence the reason I travel by train and he takes the Mercedes. I suppose I should be grateful. If I travelled by Mercedes I would never have met you. Dad does encourage me to put up ideas about the running of the company and my friend, Brian, has been trying to talk me into bringing our business to Carringtons. Dad has been reluctant to make the change from Burrows because he has been with them so long but he wants me to show initiative. I have to convince him the change is in the company's best interest. From what Brian has told me, Carringtons would be a good option. I am sure that you may have other ideas. Maybe we could discuss those over lunch as well as getting to know each other.'

Annie's mind raced. She had been so infatuated by Brian she hardly noticed Bill. Here was a handsome young man from a wealthy family who has seen her on the train and wanted to meet her. He probably had the choice of a lot of young upper-class women due to his father's position. All her previous male acquaintances were virtually people she grew up with. They were more like brothers than possible life partners. She had been so career orientated that she had shut out possible romances but now she realised that her work situation was reliant on factors outside of her control which could change at any time merely on a whim.

While she may never change completely her career focus, it was time for her to move on with her life. Bill obviously had an interest in her to shyly start the conversation, not knowing anything of her background or achievements. Regardless of how things worked out between them, if she could persuade Bill to keep the Hopwood account with her firm, potentially it could save her job.

She recognised that this was a moment in her life where her focus on work was ending and she was about to begin a new relationship with a person from a wealthy family. *This has all the makings of an Alpha Omega moment*, she thought, and in her own enthusiastic style, she was prepared to make the most of it.

JOURNEY'S END

Sue Sander

'TWENTY-FOUR hours. They have given him twenty-four hours, if that,' relayed Elizabeth down the phone, her voice eerily stoic. 'We need you home now, Cam. He needs you home.'

Cameron was at work when his mother called. She rang in between meetings whose importance seemed irrelevant now. Cameron stared at his computer screen. The adrenalin his work produced seeped out of his body, gluing him to the spot. The shrill of his mobile broke his reverie. He reached for it and hit the 'ignore' button without thought. The sounds within the surrounding office felt claustrophobic. He had to leave. He had to escape before any more demands were placed on him. This new awareness rebooted Cameron's body with purpose.

Pushing back his chair he strode towards his boss's office and entered after a brief knock. Cameron explained he needed time off, that a family member was dying and he had to go home immediately. His boss, a fair but results-driven man, raised his eyebrows at this request. A thousand reasons why this was impossible ran through his head, but looking at Cameron's face he could see the young man was already gone.

'Go. Get back as soon as you can.'

The words were barely uttered before Cameron turned and hurried back to his desk. He went to book a flight but vetoed the plan quickly. The idea of navigating airports and containing his emotions in a cabin full of strangers repulsed him. He knew driving, whilst longer, meant action. It meant he had control of something when everything else was agonisingly out of control.

Two hours later he was on the highway. He had planned to leave straight away but common sense saw him make a detour via his apartment. Cameron called in on his neighbour who agreed to collect his mail and keep an eye on the place.

The biggest delay was deciding what to pack. This seemed an insurmountable task in Cameron's fractious mind. Positioned on the edge of his bed, he found the triviality of choosing clothes his undoing. Cameron was overcome by the same inertia that had hit him after his mother's call. He knew his mind was ruminating over things like clothes rather than dealing with the big issue – going home to say goodbye to Ben.

Cameron glanced at a photo of them both, taken during a fishing trip. It was a 'selfie' taken by Cameron and appeared a little out of focus as Ben did not understand the concept. The photo had sat beside Cameron's bed for so long it had moved out of his conscious sight. Since Ben had become sick the image in the frame had taken on renewed importance. Many a night Cameron's eyelids had given in to sleep staring at the photo, filling his dreams with a kaleidoscope of memories.

Reality could wait no longer. Cameron had to leave. He threw clothes into a bag impatiently as he realised the delay the indecision had caused. He negotiated the city traffic and headed towards his childhood home. The monotony of the highway allowed his memories free rein. They delivered him back to when he first met Ben.

As an eleven-year-old boy on the cusp of adolescence, Cameron lost his father from a massive heart attack. There was no time to say goodbye. No time to whisper last messages of love. The pain of losing his father was worsened by this lack of closure. Now he faced losing another family member and he had to be there. He was determined to have the time with Ben he was denied with his father.

AFTER his father's death well-meaning relatives would tell Cameron he was now the head of the household. He had to look after his mother and younger sister, Anne. Cameron still wondered why people would place such a huge expectation on the slumped shoulders of an eleven-year-old boy. Cameron's family struggled for the next two years in a cloud of grief. Each tried their best to ignore the gaping hole in the house and in their hearts.

Around the time of his thirteenth birthday Cameron's mum Elizabeth started mentioning a friend she had met at work called Ben. Elizabeth was a nurse in a small specialised clinic in town. At first Cameron did not take much notice. At thirteen most boys were efficient at tuning into their mother's voice only when it served their needs. His mother's talk of work did not register on his radar. Eventually Cameron started to notice the excitement in Elizabeth's voice whenever she mentioned Ben. Over the last two years Cameron had tried his best to look after his mother and Anne, often denying his own grief to help dry their tears. He had become extremely protective of the shattered remains of his family and the change in his mother made him uneasy.

'I would like to talk to you both about Ben.'

Cameron remembered those words from his mother. He recalled the slow burn of anger swelling in his mind as he sat listening.

Elizabeth had met Ben's mother first during a visit to the clinic. She described how much she adored his elderly mother and her gentle nature. With each visit the trust and bond they formed delighted both.

One day Ben accompanied his mother, as the time had come where she could no longer travel alone. Elizabeth admitted there was an instant attraction between her and Ben. He shared his mother's kind nature and seemed grateful for the care Elizabeth had shown his family.

Over the weeks he started to visit her at the clinic and Elizabeth felt her feelings grow. She now wanted to introduce him to Cameron and Anne. She said it was time for the family to create new memories and hoped Ben would be part of those.

The slow burning in Cameron ignited and he ran from the room, knocking his chair over in his haste. His mother called after him, knowing even before his name left her lips that it was futile to make him listen any more. Exiting through the front door, Cameron headed down the street giving no thought to direction. He just needed space away from his mother's words. Words that meant change was upon them. Processes were in place which would see his aching heart tested again.

His mother was waiting for him when he returned. He felt calmer, the long walk releasing the anger from his body. Cameron remembered there was no long speech from her. Elizabeth simply requested him to give Ben a chance. She assured him that Ben would not replace his father, and she hoped over time they would become good friends. Still sceptical, Cameron nodded his understanding and made his way to bed.

Ben arrived to meet Cameron and Anne a fortnight later. He was as his mother had described: fair haired, brown eyes and a gentle but fun-loving nature. He quickly won Anne's affections with his playful antics. Cameron watched from a distance. He knew his mother expected him to make an effort so he feigned interest when Ben directed attention his way. Cameron felt confused as he watched Anne with Ben. As much as he enjoyed hearing her laughter and seeing her excited face, he felt a sense of betrayal at her easy acceptance of Ben.

As the weeks went by Ben continued to be a presence in their lives. He joined them on family outings and some of his belongings were moved into their home. At the time Cameron was trying to hide his true feelings behind a mask of indifference, but looking back he realised he had fooled no one.

Ben sensed Cameron's reluctance to accept him so he eased back on his overzealous attempts to engage him. Instead he sat by Cameron as he was doing his homework, quietly offering encouragement whenever Cameron looked his way. On the weekends when Cameron played social games of soccer with his friends and their dads, Ben would join Cameron's mother to watch. Whilst Elizabeth chatted, he would notice Ben observing the game with interest; his wish to join in written on his face. Sometimes Cameron would hear Ben's cries of encouragement whenever the ball was passed to him.

___oOo___

AS he drove, Cameron remembered how Ben eventually joined these games. One day he was on the sideline, the next he was running on the field as one of the team. Ben's enthusiasm made him popular with Cameron's friends and their dads. This was when Cameron's feelings towards Ben changed. Seeing Ben play Cameron felt pride and affection trickle into his heart.

As the months passed Cameron and Ben spent more time together. Cameron showed him his favourite hang outs and introduced him to more parts of his life. Ben took it all in his stride and, as Elizabeth had long ago predicated, new family memories were created.

They went camping and fishing together. Ben was encouraging as Cameron learnt to master the art of fly fishing, good naturedly jumping into the water to rescue many a lost rod. While Cameron remained close to his mum, Ben became his closest confidante. He listened as Cameron unloaded the trials that besiege a young man on his journey to adulthood. The memory of his Dad was locked in his heart but Ben had found a place there too.

___oOo___

IT was after midnight when Cameron turned into his mother's driveway. He turned off the engine and allowed the sudden quietness to engulf him. He felt calm sitting in the car, a safe cocoon protecting him from the storm his heart was soon to endure. Elizabeth was expecting his arrival. She turned on the patio light and stood waiting in the doorway. From the driveway Cameron could see her sadness. Like a default setting from childhood, seeing his mother upset overcame Cameron's own emotions and he exited the safety of the car. He greeted his mother with a hug; her tension eased as she leaned into the strong arms of her son.

'Shall we go see him now?' Elizabeth asked as she motioned towards his car. She knew her son well; he would want no delay. Cameron climbed back into the car and waited. His mother pulled the house door closed and walked around to the passenger side. Cameron hesitated before starting the engine, turning to look at his mother as she tightened the seat belt across her body. 'Is Anne coming with us?' he asked.

'Anne was with him all day, Cameron. She came home about an hour ago and has cried herself to sleep. She has said goodbye to Ben.' Cameron's mother sobbed out the last sentence as Cameron leaned across to hug her.

'Sorry Cam. I'm okay. Let's go. I'm better when I'm moving'.

The hospital car park was close to empty when they arrived. Cameron and his mother were ushered through to the room where Ben lay taking laboured breaths. Cameron shuddered at the sight of the tubes and machines attached to the altered shape of his beloved

Ben. A nurse was at the foot of the bed. She smiled when she saw Cameron and his mother enter.

'I'll leave you alone. Just call if you need me.'

Elizabeth directed Cameron to a chair near Ben's head. 'Talk to him, Cameron. He needs to hear your voice.'

Cameron studied Ben's face. A million different memories washed over him like a rain storm, soaking him with every emotion this familiar face evoked. Cameron tried many times to talk. Each time he choked on the words that seemed inadequate in his mind. How do you say goodbye to a presence in your life that loved you without question? Who loved you long before you allowed yourself to be loved? Overcome with the task of choosing the right words, Cameron laid his head on the bed. He allowed the tears to fall and his body gave in to the hopelessness of the moment. His body shook with grief. His mother gently rubbed his back.

The energy shift in the room seemed to reach Ben in his pain-induced slumber and he moaned softly. Cameron lifted his head and leaned in closer to the fragile body before him.

Ben's eyes opened and focused on Cameron. The familiar brown eyes looked deep into Cameron's and his body seem to take a deep settling breath. As Cameron returned Ben's gaze he realised no words were necessary. Ben knew what Cameron wanted to say. He had walked the same memory paths in his brain and each frame was one that included Cameron. They both knew the journey they had taken together and the unfair destination they now faced. No words were necessary. The end had come for one of them. The other had to continue on with the strength and love those memories granted.

Ben's eyes closed again. A sense of dignified finality filled the room as Ben's breaths became shallower. 'I love you, Ben.' whispered Cameron, as he stroked Ben's head. 'It's time to rest, my friend. You have a new beginning waiting for you. Our journey together has come to an end but my love for you will be eternal.'

Permission granted, the old yellow Labrador took one last shuddering breath and passed away with his adored master by his side.

Somebody's Child
Daphne Gibson

This child looks so out of place – why does she look so sad?
How did she get into this mess? Where are her Mum or Dad?
Her eyes stare at me full of pain while tears wash down her face.
She should be with her friends at school, not in this awful place.
Why does she not return to home? That's where she ought to be,
Not standing here alone to be judged now by you or me.
Why has this child gone very wrong? Life's isn't just a game.
Is it her fault she went astray? Should we not bear some blame?

His eyes glare out at us with hate, his ears adorned with rings.
Above his brow are more implants, a row of silver things.
With tattooed arms folded tight, his attitude's irate.
A young face numbed by life itself, his heart so full of hate.
What caused this anger in the lad at such an early age?
How was he hurt and just how bad? It's hard for us to gauge.
He should be joining other lads at work and fun and play,
Not getting into pain and strife, not living this way.

These children of today are lost – society's outcast
And once they wandered off the path they cannot lose their past.
They've fallen into wayward ways – they're lonely and sad.
Their pain they cannot cast away – neither the girl nor lad.
They need to try to change their lives and guidance on their way.
Let's try to find some way to help to start this plan today.
To get them help to find support before they run wild.
They could be mine –or maybe yours? – they are somebody's child.

MY FIRST PUBLIC SPEECH

Vera Murray

IT was in the 1970s. I'd done my time as a round-the-clock, full-time mother. Now I was free to get out and about. I looked for something to do. I knew the younger scene was not my cup of tea. I didn't drink alcohol, didn't smoke, use pot, and never dropped the 'F....' word.

When I read a write-up on the Portia Debating Club, a product of the women's- rights era, in which they invited only women to join, I knew that was IT. Being a good talker, and having had a lot of experience arguing with the kids, I knew I'd fit in, although I squirmed with horror at the thought of standing up alone to talk in front of people.

I joined around the middle of the year, and by late November I was looking forward to the annual Christmas dinner. Well, I was, until an upset occurred. The chosen after-dinner speaker withdrew because of an attack of laryngitis. She claimed she would not be able to speak on the night...no way. Suddenly I found everyone at the meeting had turned and was looking at ME. The silence was overwhelming.

'Oh no!' I blurted out. Somehow no-one seemed to hear me, or they were not listening. Beryl, my friend, spoke softly to me. 'Good experience. You'll have to do it some time. It may as well be now.'

'I can't,' I protested. Beryl only smiled. Others nearby smiled with her. I didn't know I had so many supporters. Of course I'm not stupid. They were relieved the finger was pointing at me, not at them. I knew that.

'Of course you can.' Beryl made an effort to soothe me. She sounded like my mother when I couldn't grasp her crocheting instructions. She then whispered, 'I'll help you.' I spluttered and pouted and protested but to no avail. 'You can't let the side down,' she said...so I was IT.

I went through days and days of thinking, working, and worrying, until the night finally arrived. With my speech written, read a thousand times, and learned by heart, I arrived at the

Sheraton Hotel in Brisbane with Beryl. My notes were clutched in one perspiring hand.

After we were seated, it seemed no time before it was my turn to speak. I looked around at the crowd before me...only forty people, but it seemed to me to be a sea of faces...with expressions of happy anticipation. They had all turned and were staring in my direction from the comfort of their little tables, away from the remains of an excellent three-course meal of choice...soup, roast chicken or duck, and delicious Christmas pudding with plenty of either cream or hot custard. The fright that now had come over me was born somewhere in the depth of my brain. It spread to my nerves. I was scared stiff I would get tongue-tied.

'No, Beryl, I can't do this. I can't possibly stand alone up there and make a speech. Halfway through I'll forget what I'm going to say,' I whispered, trembling.

'Just hold your notes in the palm of your hand and refer to them when you need to,' was Beryl's ultimatum. This was followed by a supposedly comforting pat on my shoulder.

But I knew that my hands, already doing dance steps with my stomach, would shake so much I'd never be able to focus on the words. To have any chance of reading them I'd be bobbing my head up and down in unison with my shaking hand movements.

I looked around at the staring eyes. *No! No!* screamed my mind as sheer panic struck. The words I tried to utter seemed more like shrieks.

'But you were so good when you rehearsed it with me yesterday. You knew it off pat.' Beryl was sounding more and more like my mother by the minute.

'You're my friend. I don't have to be THAT GOOD for friends,' I wailed.

I felt Beryl's hand patting one of my trembling shoulders. 'It's just stage fright. You'll be okay once you start.'

What did she know? I knew I could never begin. I'd already forgotten, not only the first line but the title and the subject as well. I rose very, very reluctantly to my feet.

'Don't forget to welcome the VIPs present, as your opening,' was Beryl's parting advice. She gave me a sudden thump on my back, which caused me to reel down between tables and up to the dais. When I got there I did remember to grin, although I stood behind the dais, shaking like a leaf. Everyone waited, expectant of hearing a speech they would enjoy.

There was not a clang of empty plates, a cough, a foot shuffle, nor the clink of emptied glasses to be heard. You could have heard a pin drop. That is, if the floor hadn't been carpeted. Even the hotel staff members present, some holding empty trays, were staring expectantly at me.

Now what is the name of the main invited guest…Cheryl? No! Ida? No, she was the guest at the birthday dinner. I opened my mouth. 'Guests, ladies and gentlemen, *I can't see any children, so no need to include children,* and …err…good evening…err…*To hell with names…*everybody.' Now I froze. *What was the title again?* I looked across at Beryl who smiled and nodded her head. She mouthed the title at me. *Oh yes.* It was *The Day I Lost My Pen.* Keep it simple, the president had told me. *What next…err…look at my notes…yes, yes.*

I started off. 'It was one of those days when all seemed lost. For the life of me, I couldn't find my pen, so I missed out on getting Prime Minister Whitlam's autograph while on a Women's Year event in Canberra.'

My mind suddenly went blank. *To hell with trying to remember it all.*

I tightly clutched the notes I now held close up to my face. I had taken off my glasses earlier so as to appear more glamorous, it being Christmas and all. The words were blurred but I still managed to read them…poker-faced and monotonously I felt sure. The last words of my talk…'and so I found my pen, hiding in the wheelie-bin. No doubt some gold pen owner found my chewed plastic pen and discarded it quickly.'

What do I do now…bow?…say thank-you? I stared dumbly back at the guests who sat in a silence that seemed to me judgemental. Helplessly I looked over at Beryl. She had begun to clap madly. Everyone else joined her and kept it up. *They don't seem to want to stop clapping. I must have done all right.*

Wow…I'll volunteer to speak again next year.

I BELIEVE IN GHOSTS

Suzanne Cowell

'CAN you and Jess come over tonight? I have something I want you to see?' Shane's voice sounded strange, a bit off-beat.

The young couple made the short drive to Shane and Libby's unit a few kilometres away. On arrival, their best friends seemed a little edgy. They were ushered into the lounge room where Shane promptly produced photographs taken on their Sunday outing.

Rod and Jess glanced through the photographs, then came to a halt. They looked up to see their friends watching them closely. Most of the snaps showed four people having fun, with Rod's car featured in the majority of them. However two photographs stood out eerily from the rest.

The pictures were of Rod alone with his new car. But he wasn't alone. One taken with Rod standing in front of the bright red car, arms folded in a tough-guy stance, showed a ghostly image slightly behind and above him. Without a doubt it was the face and shoulders of a man. It was looking down towards Rod, the expression on the face, one of anger.

In the second photo, Rod was standing at the back of the car, and in this one, a woman's face was evident. She appeared to be standing right beside Rod. Although also looking down, maybe at the car, she looked sad, perhaps even crying. Silence filled the room as the two young couples stared in disbelief at these two images. There had been no fog or mist the day of the picnic at Mary Caincross Park, no camp-fires lit anywhere near them. The apparitions were revealed only in these two photographs.

This event occurred after Rod saw the advertisement in the Saturday Classifieds.

FOR SALE 1966 Chevrolet Impala SS Convertible. V8 396/325 HP. Column shift 3-speed manual. Fire Engine Red. Red leather upholstery, black top. Immaculate condition. One owner only. $25,000 Phone 47489211 to inspect.

Rod looked into the yard of the little fifties' style house, as his mate Shane turned off the ignition. Thirty-eight Chandler Street was a small home, neatly painted, surrounded by a well-kept yard. They got out of Shane's car and entered the property through the open drive-way gate. Shane stopped at the bottom of the five steps as Rod went up to the front door. He was about to knock when it opened.

A slim frail man about eighty met Rod's look with faded grey eyes. Though lined with age his face appeared younger than the worn body. His hair was thick, cut short, light grey turning white.

'I'm Rod Lemke, I called yesterday. I've come to look at the Chevy.'

The old man seemed to be assessing Rod, as he extended his right arm for the usual handshake between men. 'Hello, I'm Bill - we'll go out to the garage.'

Bill stepped onto the front landing and motioned Rod back down the stairs. The two young men followed him down the driveway alongside the house, to a garage at the back of the property, where he unlocked the timber doors and opened them wide.

Rod's heart skipped a few beats. There she was, the 1966 eight-cylinder Chevrolet Impala. His dream car. It was spotless, the chrome work glistened even in the shady garage. The stunning red paintwork sent a ripple of excitement through him.

Old Bill looked on, as the young man gently caressed the leather upholstery and steering wheel.

'Do you mind if I look under the bonnet?' Rod asked.

Bill handed him the keys to the car. 'Feel free, I'll be on the front veranda when you're done.'

Rod and Shane checked out the engine, radiator and water hoses, the level and colour of oil on the dip-stick, the exhaust pipe, tyres and instrument panel. The body work showed no signs of rust, dodgy repairs or shoddy paint job. They lay on the ground, heads beneath the car and looked up for any signs of oil leaks. There were none. Rod turned the key to check out the lights. The Chevrolet was in perfect condition.

'I'm buying it,' Rod stated.

Shane agreed with his best friend's decision. They closed the garage doors and returned to the front veranda, where Bill sat on a squatter's chair. He didn't get up as Rod came up the stairs.

'Twenty-five thousand was the price, right?'

Old Bill nodded. It was obvious Bill was a man of few words.

'She's worth every cent,' Rod said quietly.

Something in Bill's eyes flickered as he seemed to pay particular attention to Rod's demeanour. The grey eyes watered as Bill stood up. He shook the younger man's hand, his grasp firm and strong, like that of a much younger man.

'I know you'll take good care of it,' he murmured, a slight tremble in his voice.

'Is a bank cheque ok? I'll need your full name for it and come by with it Friday afternoon, if that suits you?'

'Kilkenny, Bill Kilkenny.'

Not another word was uttered, although Bill's face conveyed a look of satisfaction – or was it relief?

True to his word, Rod had Shane drop him off Friday afternoon with the bank cheque. He handed it to Bill and received a hand-written receipt and paperwork for the transfer of registration, along with the keys. Attached to them was a St Christopher medal, the Patron Saint of travellers. The medal had not been on the key ring when Rod inspected the car.

The convertible was parked in the driveway. Rod got in, heart thumping with excitement as he turned on the ignition. The engine sprang to life with a soothing rumble from beneath the massive bonnet. He gave it a few minutes to warm up, then, hands trembling, he eased the gear-stick back towards him and up, putting the car into reverse. Slowly he backed the Chevy out of the yard and into the street. He glanced to his left but the old man was nowhere to be seen. Gently Rod moved the lever down through neutral, into first gear. Euphoria overwhelmed him as he drove out of Chandler Street.

On arrival at the little house he and Jess rented, Shane, Libby and Jess were waiting, cold bubbly and beer in the fridge. The two girls oohed and aahed as they appreciated the beauty of the flashy convertible. When Rod opened the large boot, the girls were overawed.

'It's big enough to take a double mattress, though you would have to put the spare on the ground,' Libby exclaimed.

Rod wrapped an arm around Jesse's shoulders and hugged her close.

'I owe you big time,' he murmured in her ear.

Jess embraced him in return. 'Not really. Your dreams are my dreams as well. It was meant to be.'

The twenty-five thousand had created a massive hole in their savings. Their chance of buying a home was put off even longer. Jess knew it had been Rod's childhood dream to buy such a car, and when the ad appeared in the paper, she had urged him to call the number and go to check it out. Her sixth sense told her it was the right thing to do.

The cork flew from the bottle of Asti Spumante. Jess and Libby's glasses filled. Rod and Shane broke open the first of many beers they would drink that afternoon. An outing was planned between drinks and laughter. On Sunday, the four of them would drive up to Mary Caincross Park to have a picnic lunch amongst the trees.

Sunday's weather was perfect for their first trip in Rod's new car. Clear blue skies announced a fine April day, and, once free of slower city traffic, they cruised up the highway, an exhilarating breeze whipping through their hair. Less than an hour later they reached their destination. Rod parked the car a little away from the trees, not wanting bird droppings on his prized possession. Jess and Libby spread out the picnic blanket and unloaded the Esky from the boot. Red wine poured into glasses and they settled themselves in the shade, taking in the scent of the fresh country air and the peace and quiet that surrounded them.

As they did so, Shane took numerous photographs of Rod, either sitting in his newly acquired set of wheels, and standing proudly beside, in front of, and behind it, arms folded, a smug look on his face. There was no denying Rod was ecstatic over his new possession.

The foursome spent a relaxing day, eating, drinking, and enjoying the outdoors and one another's company. As much as Rod enjoyed a beer or two, today was not the day for it. He was on a high just looking at his new car, so happily settled for Coke, while the others knocked over a few alcoholic drinks. Everyone posed around the Chevy and photographs were taken throughout the day. Close to sunset, picnic gear was packed into the huge boot of the car and the four of them settled comfortably into the soft leather seats for the journey home.

Three days later Rod got the phone call from Shane.

Everyone who viewed the images came up with their own theories as to the presence of the two ghosts. Most believed the car had previously belonged to the male figure.

Was he angry Rod now owned and drove his car, when he was no longer able to?

And what of the woman's sadness? Was she the girlfriend or wife, grieving the loss of her loved one? Had they both died as a result of an accident involving the vehicle? Did the look on old Bill's face belie the fact he was relieved to be rid of the car, or were his emotions torn by having to part with it? The car may have been the remaining possession of a departed loved one.

The immaculate appearance of the convertible seemed to rule out any accident, in fact it was in showroom condition. Had it been driven at all, since the sixties?

Rod is now trying to uncover the car's history, to find some answers to all the questions the photographs have produced.

Author's Note

The basis of this story is a true event that took place. I, and many others, have viewed these two ghostly images, clearly visible in the two photographs.

Red Flames
Daphne Gibson

RED FLAMES
Leap-frog in red-hot bush fires
Dance and devour all the trees,
Fast changing all that it touches to red
Like passion aroused and inflamed.

Red traffic lights
signal all to stop there
to wait for a green light…then go.
Like love unreturned, it's a sign to desist
before raw emotions take hold.

Red roses
a symbol of Cupid's bow strike
is felt by all those in love's throes
sent as a message to one who's desired
by a lover whose heart is afire.

Red lips
make lovers afire with desire
to be with the one they adore
but love unrequited turns red to blue
when emotions glare out of control.

Red eyes
A result of a need unfulfilled
And tears shed because of love's loss
That pain in our hearts
Like the blood in our veins
Makes our world burn with.
RED FLAMES

FIRST DO NO HARM

Sarah L. Wilson

OMEGA was fuming. The staff had caught on quickly and were giving her a wide berth, none willing to risk her wrath. She stalked the halls, dragging her gloved, nine-year-old hand along the walls, daring someone to tell her off. Her eyes moved to anyone she came across with an unwavering glare. *Cross me,* they challenged, *say just one word wrong, give me an excuse.* But as always when trouble came her way, Omega was left alone.

People, admittedly, had never been her strong point. Even before her 'talents' began to emerge, she had known she was different. It was like a stone in her heart, her own inbuilt warning system. You are dangerous. They are fragile. Leave them be.

And she did, especially after that time with her baby brother... a game of make-believe hospital that turned into a real family trip to the ICU. Minus Omega of course.

She had been called Rosanna then, Rose for short. Rose had liked books and sunsets and drawing. Omega had not been outside in weeks, and she did not draw. But at least here she had her own personal library and hours a day to utilise it.

Omega's path led her to the cafeteria. She began to trace around its perimeter, wiping her hand along the pristine white walls, leaving a grey trail filled with cracks. Each lap made the groove slightly deeper. The angry thoughts bumped against each other in her mind, bustling and jostling until she felt the drip from her nose. She cried out in alarm, running for the tissue box on the counter whilst cupping her hand under her nose to catch the crimson drops.

'Are you alright?'

Omega turned. The speaker was a girl, *the girl.* She looked about the same age and size as Omega, but with platinum hair, shockingly pale eyes and tanned skin. Omega had porcelain skin but was dark everywhere else. It was like they were negatives of each other, or the second player in a videogame. Same design, different colour palette.

'I guess. It happens a lot when I'm mad.'

The girl cocked her head. 'Why?'

'I don't know. It just does.'

'No, I meant, why are you mad?'

'None of your business.'

'Fine.' The girl paused, chewing on her glove. Omega was pleasantly surprised to see the new girl had the ugly standard-issue pair. *Her* gloves were custom-made of soft leather. 'I could fix it,' the girl continued, 'That's what I do; fix things.'

Before Omega could object the girl removed her gloves and placed a hand on Omega's nose.

Omega flinched and grabbed the girl's wrist. 'Don't!'

The girl just smiled like she'd done this a hundred times before, which she probably had. The ones with useful skills always got practice, got to go on outings. 'It's fine, you can trust me. My name's Alpha, by the way.'

Alpha continued smiling for about ten seconds before her expression twisted and changed into one of considerable pain. She pulled away and Omega let her go. They both looked down to Alpha's wrist, which now sported an ugly graze in the shape of a hand.

The pale-skinned girl swallowed, looked Alpha in the eye and said, 'My name's Omega, and that's what I can do, with the gloves still on.'

OMEGA had only learnt about the new girl the previous night. The head researcher, Milton, had drawn the short straw and landed the job of introducing the idea to her.

He walked into Omega's room with as much courage as he could muster. He very nearly tripped on his first step, both from nerves and the piles of books scattered across the floor.

'Hey, guess what?' he said, largely keeping his voice from cracking.

Omega was lying on the bed reading, so she didn't even look up. 'What?' she grunted.

'Omega.' Milton's voice was firm. There was a strict code of conduct around the staff, although Omega still got away with more than anyone else in the Institute.

She looked up, jerking her head around so that her hair flipped comically. She plastered a cheesy grin across her face. 'What?' she repeated an octave higher. She was trying to irritate him. It was working.

'There's another little girl moving in tomorrow,' he said, massaging his temples.

This wasn't all that novel to Omega, who turned back to her book. 'Whatever.'

Milton sucked in a tentative breath. 'Into your room.'

She whipped back around. 'No.'

'Yes. Omi, you need a friend. You can't stay hidden in here forever.'

'Yes I can.' She fiddled with her gloves, as she always did when she was anxious. She tried to ignore the terror in Milton's eyes. 'I'd like that, to stay hidden forever.'

'I'm sorry, but the decision's been made.'

Omega's face changed instantly into a scowl. 'I don't care! It's not fair! It's never fair!'

He tried to control his rising panic. 'Omi, you are the child and I am the adult. And I say that having another little girl, one who understands what you're going through, will do you good.'

'No friends! No little girls! No! No! NO!' She was pressing her palms against her ears now, her eyes squeezed shut. Milton did not even hesitate as he raced for the door, bolting it closed behind him.

Omega screamed. She could feel it in every part of her body; the air vibrated through her ribcage and throat, bursting out her wide-open mouth like an untamed animal. She felt the hate, the fear, the anger that were always sitting in the bottom of her stomach come spewing forth.

First it hit the wall in front of her. The mirror dissolved to silver dust, books were thrown from their shelves, and cracks began to form in the plaster. This just angered Omega more. That mirror was brand new. Those books were her favourites. That paintjob was the best in a long time. And now it was all broken and warped, as everything always ended up. Her screams became stronger and more urgent.

The surge of energy continued to spread. Like an invisible hand, it tore the sheets from her bed, ripped the mobile from the ceiling, knocked the glass of water off the dresser. And still she screamed.

A tornado of objects formed in the centre of the room. Chunks of plaster began to the break off the walls, sucked into the rotating mess. Omega could feel the dust in her throat. She could hear the din of various objects smashing together. She knew the noise she was making was piercing, hellish. She kept pushing, as if she could purge everything if she just kept going long and hard enough.

But she couldn't. Her throat was killing her from both the pressure and the dust. She desperately needed a proper breath. The noise changed steadily from a screech to cry, then from a cry to a final huff of air as she dissolved into sobs, her mouth still open but now turned down at the sides. Tears snaked their way down her cheeks, mingling with the layer of perspiration formed from the exertion.

Omega was tired now. So tired. She just wanted someone to come scoop her up, hold her close and tell her it would all be okay. But only good girls got that. Good girls had parents and friends and little brothers who could still walk. Good girls had people who would sing them to sleep at night and let them read under the covers and never ever made them cry.

But Omega knew she was not a good girl. She was bad; very, very bad.

ALPHA'S horrified cry had drawn a crowd of staff members ready to bring comfort and specially prepared salves, but no amount of coaxing could bring an apology from her new roommate. Instead she remained unresponsive, silently staring at Alpha's wrist as the wound healed.

The combination of Alpha's abilities and the lab-prepared ointment made the healing significantly faster than any ordinary person would have expected. Still, Alpha had never seen a wound close so slowly. As if the situation needed more discomfort, she could feel Omega's eyes boring into the back of her head. At one point the intensity of the stare was so great that a staff member noticed and snapped, 'Back off, Omega! It won't work while you're here.'

Omega took a step backwards, apparently unfazed by his sharpness. Once Omega was out of range a golden glow encased Alpha's trembling hand, a clear signal that she was healing at full speed.

'You know, I won't be able to hurt her again if she's in her old ward,' Omega said casually, 'Maybe it will be better if we move her back now.'

Alpha turned towards where Omega was brooding, but Milton interjected. 'Don't worry about her, just focus on that hand,' he said to Alpha.

'If it's easier we can wait until tomorrow. She can sleep in my room overnight and be transferred in the morning.'

Alpha's eyes remained concentrated on her hand but she turned the rest of her attention to Omega. 'That's not going to work. I wasn't in a ward before, and I can't go back where I came from.'

Omega licked her lips. 'Why not?'

The golden glow ceased. Alpha sighed and gave her wrist a once-over. 'Why do you think?' Her voice was tired, belonging to someone much older. 'Because families suck.'

Omega's face fell sympathetically. 'It's alright for you, you can fix things. Bet they just wanted to give you to someone who understood your condition better. Bet they thought there was no other option. Bet they'll start missing you really soon, realise what a mistake this was and come to get you.'

The words hung sadly in the air and both girls knew it was a bittersweet lie, one they had both countless times heard before.

'That's enough, Omega,' Milton said, not liking the direction the conversation had taken. 'Alpha is now a permanent resident and you will behave yourself around her. And – he threw Alpha her gloves – *both* of you will keep your gloves on at all times.'

There was the distinct sound of cracking concrete as Omega gritted her teeth. 'Yes, sir. Whatever you say.'

_____oOo_____

THEY were outside playing when it happened. It was a cloudy spring morning, about a month after Alpha had first arrived. To the dismay of both girls, the staff had insisted they stay wrapped up. The small playground was sparse and brambly, with only spartan pieces of play equipment.

They were set to have an hour outside that day. The girls rarely played together, Alpha preferring conversation with invisible friends and Omega to build small villages out of sticks.

Today, however, was different. Alpha took up her usual spot on the roof of the creaking jungle-gym, but Omega just stood as close to the inside doorway as possible. At first Alpha thought it might have been the cold; there was a strong wind blowing, and she herself had never been as sensitive to sensation as other people. But a few of the clouds parted and even she could feel the unseasonal warmth. Alpha was sure the cold was not the cause.

Alpha dropped down from her roof-top perch. She felt her foot crunch uncomfortably and reached down to hold it in position while it took a moment to heal. It was a bad habit and she had been told off many times for it, but it took longer to climb down 'safely' than to jump and risk a few seconds' recovery.

Alpha walked across the playground, feeling her tendons re-discover their purpose in life. Omega looked up sullenly as her roommate drew near. 'Why are you sad?' said Alpha.

'I'm not sad. I'm cross,' said Omega.

'Yes you are,' Alpha reached out and touched Omega's cheek to confirm. 'You're very sad.'

Omega slapped her hand down. 'Stop that! I'll take my gloves off!'

'I'm not afraid of you,' Alpha said, before running her tongue across her teeth. That was her only nervous tic, the only reading one would get on a great actor.

'Yes you are. And if you don't stop asking so many questions I'll come over there and I'll…' Omega continued glaring even as her words trailed off.

Alpha smoothed her dress down, trying not to look frazzled. It was a challenge; Omega was intimidating to adults twice her size. 'Why are you sad, Omi?'

Omega laughed bitterly. 'You sound like our Psych.'

Alpha bit her lip and tucked a thin lock of white hair behind her ear. 'Why, Omi?' she repeated calmly.

'It's not Omi!' Omega snapped, her dark eyes full of fire. 'Don't say it short like it's a name, because it's not. It's a title. It means I'm the end. It means I break everything I touch. It means you should be very, very, very scared of me. But it is not. My. Name. MY NAME IS ROSE!'

Alpha stood still and blinked a couple of times. There was a thick scorch mark across the concrete from underneath Omega's feet to about an inch away from Alpha's sandals. To Omega's frustration, it did not touch her. Alpha's healing cancelled out whatever harm Omega tried to inflict. But that was not reassuring enough to stop Alpha from flinching. She could still feel the instinctively generated power coursing through her veins.

There was a silence between them and Alpha could see Omega's lip tremble, although she was fighting it ferociously. Apparently unwilling to bear the humiliation of breaking down in front of her one peer, Omega tried to push past Alpha, only to find herself jerked back by the cuff of her jacket.

Omega pulled back, her eyes already glassed over with tears. 'Let go of me!'

'Omeg...' Alpha stopped herself, 'Rose, I had no idea. I never got a proper name. I didn't know you might...'

'Just leave me alone!' Omega gave an almighty tug, freeing her sleeve from Alpha's grasp. She used the momentum to pivot around, and was sprinting through the building before Alpha could even blink. All she registered was the sound of Omega's sobs echoing through the hallway.

___oOo___

LATER that night – probably close to midnight, although there were no clocks in the room to confirm – Omega woke up shrieking.

Alpha, who had always been a light sleeper, rolled over to the edge of her top bunk and hung her head down to look. 'You 'kay, Rose?' she whispered, her voice slurred with sleepiness.

'Yair.' Omega was definitely awake. She looked even paler than usual and even in the dark Alpha could see she was shaking. 'I always get bad dreams when it's hot.'

'It's hot?'

'Boiling.' Omega said. Alpha removed a glove in a vain effort to confirm this herself.

'Can't you tell?'

'No. Don't 'member the last time I felt hot.' Alpha squinted sleepily. 'Last time I felt much of anything.'

Omega sat up, trying to untangle herself from a wad of sheets as she spoke. 'That's why it took so long for me to hurt you?'

'S'pose. Dunno.' Alpha had not realised her reaction was unusual. She figured all the usual sensation-free rules didn't apply to Omega's touch.

Omega finally won her battle with the bed sheets and lay back down. Alpha gave an involuntary sigh.

'What?' Omega said.

'Nothing.'

'No, what?' Omega propped herself up on her elbows so she could see Alpha properly, if still upside-down.

'You'll think I'm a big baby,' Alpha said.

'I already do. What were you thinking out?'

Alpha sighed again. 'My sister, how she used to come into my room and sing to me when I couldn't sleep. I wish she was here.'

Omega nodded. 'My daddy used to wrap me in a blanket so he could rock me to sleep without getting hurt. I miss him too.' Omega picked at the tips of her gloves. 'Miss having someone who wasn't afraid of me.'

There was a moment of silence. 'You could take them off,' Alpha said, pointing.

'Yeah, right.'

'When was the last time you touched something properly, without the gloves?'

'I don't remember… but I don't anymore.' Omega was irritated now. 'I break things.'

'Well I can't feel, and you can. I'm not going to let them take that away from you. Come here.' Alpha held out her ungloved hand. 'You break. I fix. We'll cancel each other out, right?'

Hesitantly Omega met her gaze. With a wave of pure, blind courage she ripped off the gloves. Immediately the room was filled with a silver glow. 'This is stupid,' Omega said.

There were golden sparks dancing across Alpha's palm. 'Come on, before we wake up the whole department.'

'What if I hurt you?'

'Are you trying to hurt me?'

'No, of course not.'

With that, Alpha pressed her hand to Omega's. At first it was worse than anything she'd felt ever in her short life. Every nerve-ending was set ablaze, and she bit into one glove to keep from crying out. After a second, it subsided, as the golden sparks grew to match the encompassing silver light.

Meanwhile Omega, who had at first been caught off guard, frowned at the new sensation. She moved her fingers cautiously around Alpha's hand, absorbing every nook and cranny.

'What's it like?'

'It's… awesome.' Omega looked up. 'Are you afraid?'

'No. I thought you hated me, but I wasn't scared.' Alpha shifted her hand to grasp Omega's. 'Truce?'

Omega smiled, her face lit up by the shifting lights. 'Truce.'

And, gloves off, they shook on it.

Light of Hope
Bakthi Ross

You come out of the earth,
Look for that light of life.
You live for a day.
Die the next day like a mushroom.

Light of life you never see,
All the things you hoped for,
You will never achieve.
You enjoy that moment of fun and laughter,
In the darkness of that dark cloud of emotions.

Life seems meaningless without that light of hope,
You live in that darkness.
When you couldn't see that light of life,
You curl up and die.

Living in the darkness is much better.
Because you do not have to face that light.
You made it dark by crossing that line of conscience.

You could never overcome that conscience.
You dark it.
You hide it.
But when you are alone it resurfaces again.

You feel happy when your mind is clouded.
When your mind is clear,
You hate the world,
You ridicule other people,
You make jokes.
Because you cannot overcome that conscience.

You feel stupid,
You feel fear,
You feel emotionally abused,
Because of that conscience.

You feel scared of the life,
Once you felt sorry for the poor,
Now you wish you could kill them all.
Under the cloud of darkness,
You feel anger and hatred.

THE CHILD AND THE DANCING LLAMA

David MacLaughlin

JOHN sat back and was watching the English countryside from the comfort of the rail train as it sped from London to York in under 1 hour 40 mins. He grinned to himself as his home town Tilt Train took as long to get from Pomona to Brisbane and the distance was so much shorter than his present journey. His mind was racing, as the last few days had been hectic.

He had been lucky enough to get a trip to the UK and his assignment was to obtain a human-interest story to fill the summer editions of his employer's newspaper. Before he left Brisbane he was thinking along the lines of a story titled with a beginning and an end such as Alpha & Omega. He chuckled to himself as every story has a beginning and an end.

Everyone was on holiday back home, not quite true, but it was a quiet period for newspaper sales and anything to increase sales was always welcomed by his boss.

He had left his wife and two young boys happily ensconced in a London hotel near St. Pancreas where he had caught the train. He had bought his ticket online and got it printed quickly through a ticket machine in the busy station. He knew how to get around Central Station back home but he found St Pancras bewildering at first until he learnt how to follow the signs and bulletin boards to locate his train and platform. He was impressed by the ease of getting on the train. It left right on time and soon he was sipping a coffee and watching the winter landscape on his 323km journey.

The English now even made a flat white which was unheard of a few years before. For some reason a flat white cost more than a cappuccino.

He could have chosen any train but this was a direct service and that suited him. It was winter just after Christmas so there were no leaves on the trees but the sunlight showed the passing towns, villages, lakes and rivers which comprised the patchwork beauty of the countryside. His eyes and quick reporter's brain noticed a number of billowing towers of smoke the further north the train travelled. Suddenly he realised that there were nuclear power plants. *A sign of things to come back home*, he thought. The contrast between nature and the man-made generators using nuclear fuel occupied his mind. What a contrast, he mused.

He knew York was a former Viking settlement, steeped in history. He had been before and seen the usual sights and buildings of this still-beautiful cathedral city but the human-interest story angle was eluding him. Interviewing crusty old characters in rural England had been done to death and his boss would not be impressed if nobody wanted to read the article and thus sell fewer newspapers. Maybe an animal story, with a cat and dog could be more interesting than the human characters he might interview. The English treat their pets like humans. *Cats and dogs can enter butcher shops and cafes*, John was thinking, which was something he did not do all that much.

He was looking forward to York and to re-connect with its winding lanes, the majesty of the cathedral, the beauty of the river meandering through the city and its still intact walled area. He had arranged to stay outside York in a village which was so very Old English. Not old in the sense of antiquity but that every building in the village was owned by the one landlord. A sort of throwback to the landholders of feudal England. Families had been farming there for generations.

Leaving the train station he caught one of the many waiting taxies. With some light luggage on board he sat and watched many of the tourist sights of York as the cab wound its way to his abode about 15km away. He had an urge to turn his head and shoulders and he caught sight of a bike rider through the back windscreen of the taxi. *That face,* he thought, *I have seen it before in outback Oz.* He felt uneasy for a few seconds.

He had been to the village before but could not remember where Manor Lodge was. After a few attempts the taxi located it at the end of a long lane and left him to his fate.

Manor Lodge had originally been the gate keeper's lodge to the real manor house up the lane way. The whole property had been sold and was used as a residence with the stables converted to rentable lodges. It looked amazing to John. This stone building and rambling former stables were turned into a place for a family as well as rentable accommodation, farm style.

York has not got the ideal climate. On his arrival the wind was biting and light rain had started to fall.

He was not alone. As it was after the Christmas season, the owner Jean's mother and son were staying. A young nine-year old Aussie girl and her mother were staying as well. The nine-year old Vicki was full of fun, mischief and had a bright cheeky inquisitive face. Her working mother was hoping for a quiet rest as she slumped onto the couch but her daughter would not be so accommodating. *Maybe I could use the girl in my story.* John was starting to think again, which was rarely a good thing.

Soon the host arranged a lunch cooked by her son, a professional rugby player. Then everyone sat around the glowing wood-burning fireside and chatted. The girl was restless. The host decided a walk in the rain and cold was a good idea and the girl agreed.

All rugged up, John joined them outside for what he expected would be a short uneventful stroll through muddy fields.

He had not realised that the manor lodge where he was staying was near Castle Howard, the heritage-listed historical estate which had been used in many English movies. Trudging along a path through the middle of a field, his host Jean pointed out the famous estate over the crest of a hill. *Wow*, thought John, *maybe that would be his human-interest story.*

As he was day dreaming, the nine-year old girl laughed loudly. He turned around and saw right beside him a friendly donkey looking into the kid's face. *A donkey indeed is interesting*, John thought, *but the place is full of them.* He smiled. As he turned to continue the walk in the windy but clear cold day, another yell came from the girl. This time he was surprised.

Beside the donkey loomed this long-necked creature swaying its head and looking directly at John. ' Hell,' he gasped, "it's a llama." "What is it doing here?"

Jean the host replied it was one of a couple. 'They are bred next door to us.'

The llama was swaying its long neck and looked well fed in its shiny wool body covering. John was taken aback completely. A llama in this part of the world, how un-English is that? The llama, wearing a beautiful warm wool coat, looked aghast at the girl who was laughing and excited at seeing such a creature up close.

Jean's two dogs were scampering on the horizon and not a bit interested in this tall swaying creature. However, something attracted their attention. John noticed a shape near the hedges where the dogs were barking. The barking stopped and the dogs headed back to the group. John thought no more of the incident.

He was elated; he now had his human-interest story. He would embellish just a little. Maybe suggest that the llama was wild, had escaped from a local Howard Castle zoo and was looking to eat up the girl when it was foiled in its attempt by the donkey which bit the llama's bottom and sent it packing back to the zoo. The zoo could be located in or around Castle Howard Estate Theme Park. John's mind was getting ahead of itself but he enjoyed a bit of day dreaming, knowing that the sub-editor would see through his mixture of fact and fiction.

It was good to return to the warmth of the wood fire and thaw out his cold face and hands. The two dogs had scampered back and went straight to the dry part of the former manor stables. The llama and donkey were nowhere to be seen.

Later when everyone had gone to bed John was sorting out in his mind the story he would send to earn his keep. It was windy and the nearly full moon was shining through one of his bedroom windows. He was on the ground floor and he could see the outline of the nearby trees swaying in the breeze. The bedroom beside him was occupied by the nine-year-old Oz schoolgirl who talked a lot.

Suddenly he heard a loud scream and he looked out the window. What he saw surprised him just a little. There was the llama with neck outstretched standing at the next bedroom window and waving its body to and fro. John jumped out of bed and went to the girl's bedroom next door. Her door was wide open and she had jumped onto the top of her bed as if it was a trampoline and was laughing and waving to the llama. The tall white llama was swaying his head in time to her gyrating on top of the bed. 'Wow I love this place,' she exclaimed. 'The llama is so much fun he wants to dance with me!'

All of a sudden the llama turned tail and disappeared into the fields beyond Manor Lodge. He had not even disturbed the dogs. Maybe he had visited the Lodge before and they were used to his comings and goings.

John knew he had the basis of his fair dinkum pommy human-interest story. A wonderful stone building set in rural northern England, exotic animals like the llama wandering loose, a wild windy moonlit night, and plenty of creaking doors when the llama looked into the kid's bedroom. *Now it's time to relax and have a shot of hot claret*, John thought, as the rest of the household had calmed down and gone back to bed.

John lay on his bed and felt warm and comfortable after a couple shots of port from Portugal. He was thinking about the events of the day and the glimpse of a face he had seen when he had been investing local political intrigue in outback Queensland.

Yawning, he wandered over to the window and peered out at the huge oak tree. A face looked up at him, and he nearly wet himself through sheer fright. It was the same face he had seen from the taxi window. In a flash it disappeared. He needed another port now. Not only had he his fuzzy English human-interest story, he had a `crazy' chasing him around this former feudal village.

Maybe, the Vikings had come back to haunt the place. He knew he had his story *Alpha & Omega*. But now he had the beginnings of another plot. It was Alpha all over again.

WITH EVERY GOODBYE YOU LEARN

Judy Boyd

PENELOPE swung her car into the driveway, her adrenalin rush compensating for the frustration of bumper to bumper homeward-bound Friday afternoon traffic. She could not wait to tell Donald about her coup. At last, months of networking, negotiating and support from the local medical centre, had paid off. The Hospital Board had allotted her two rooms in a new wing for her physiotherapy practice, with a view to this becoming its own Department. Her wildest dream had come true.

Inside the neat little unit that they shared and with no response to her excited 'Donald, guess what!' she became aware of unfamiliar gaps in her surrounds, and an eerie silence. A large envelope lay in the centre of the dining table. Catching her breath, she tore it open to read:

'Dear Penny,

By the time you read this I will be back in the city. I have tried to talk to you but your professional dream just would not let me in, so it got to the point that I had no alternative but to give up. I have met someone else who puts relationships before ambition and with whom I am sure I can be happy. I do not for one minute, regret our three and a half years together, but I, too, must live my dream. This is not negotiable. Please do not try to contact me.

Fondly, Donald.'

Suddenly she became aware that every trace of him had disappeared. It was as if he had never existed.

Feeling utterly numb, she collapsed into an easy chair. How could this have happened? She had been aware of a coolness between them for a while now and had resolved to attend to this once she was set up. Never in her wildest dreams had she seen this coming. Their beginning had been so needy that she felt that they would go on forever. How could she have been so stupid? Her tears flowed. She wanted him, needed him to share in her hour of triumph.

She spent the next week alternating between wallowing in her grief and acknowledging her bright professional future. Then, in her trademark spirit of perseverance, she made her fall-back position the restart of her social life with the Environmental Protection Society to which she had had a loose connection in the past.

In time the hurt did fade and she found herself responding to the advances of an earnest young Park Ranger, Tim, who, although largely humourless, impressed her with his single-minded commitment to the cause. He became her buffer against loneliness.

After a while his intense dedication became irksome and she slowly came to realize that a man without a sense of humour was not for her. The relationship withered on the vine and he, too, left which brought relief, rather than grief, she was pleased to note.

Despite these rejections, she felt reasonably good about herself. She was a routine blonde, not beautiful, but with a generous mouth and laughing eyes in a slim, but well-proportioned figure. Being a star in her work-day world gave her the confidence to be optimistic about her future. It was in this state of mind that she came across Jack.

She remembered their first meeting clearly. She was having dinner at the Bowls Club with the Environmental Protection Group.

Bob said, 'Jack, we need another boat for Sunday's work party. How about helping out? We're going to bury a dead horse at the new Environmental Park at Mission Point and we can only get there by sea.'

Jack threw back his head and let out a roar of laughter that rippled the tee shirt covering his ample belly. 'Well, if that isn't the ultimate hair shirt for you greenies. But you know that my interest in the environment doesn't extend more than twenty feet in from the shore.'

He came, of course. The lure of an equine interment and an Esky full of home brew was irresistible. It was an hilarious day with this conservationally irreverent bull of a man the dominant character in an assortment of Park Rangers and volunteers who were delighted at the proclamation of the new Park.

She found herself drawn to this unlikely man. He was about her own height and solidly built, with a face that was homely and a crooked nose that gave him a kind of rugged geniality. On the surface he was an avowed hedonist who owed no allegiance to any group or cause. At the same time, his gentle put-down of conservationist pretensions with wisdom and wit suggested a warm and caring man at heart. In another life he had worked as a Patrol Officer in New Guinea and was a lay expert on the rare neurological disorder, kuru.

Their paths crossed again a few weeks later when he was referred to her by his doctor for an aggravated shoulder injury. After the third treatment session she breached professional boundaries by discreetly angling for a date but he remained impervious to her overtures. However, her mind was made up. It was time to take a risk.

She sought him out and invited him to share a meal with her at the Club. It was something of a surprise when he accepted her invitation, but so began an initially occasional, but later more frequent, meal at the Bowls Club on Cheap Tuesday nights. She spoke of her interest in kuru from University days and he rounded this out with his own lived experiences.

On personal matters he was much more coy. He described himself as a 'marital reject' but did not expand on this. There was an unspoken understanding that personal relationships were not conversational currency in their light-hearted, dinner-time conversation where he was polite and tactfully incurious. It was their shared belief that it was never too late to have a happy childhood that filtered through their social comments on the absurdities of the here and now, where they were on safer ground.

He rekindled her interest in fishing which offered opportunities for brief physical contact which she found electrifying. She was sure that it meant something to him as well but his tools of self-protection were avoidance and self-control which made him more attractive still.

They fell into an easy friendship which was high in humour but light on any real intimacy. That was fine for now for, although she wanted more, she could afford to wait. After all, her parents married in haste and certainly repented at leisure with her mother now an angry, frustrated and bitter woman and her father as emotionally distant as anyone could be. Of one thing Penelope was sure, this was not going to happen to her.

And so their Indian summer proceeded – but not for much longer.

On the sixth-month anniversary of their meeting, and after a particularly merry meal, they were having coffee when the bartender called out, 'Someone here to see you, Jack.' Penelope, who had her back to the entrance to the dining room, was surprised to see Jack's face become drained of colour as he got up to go to the door.

She turned to see who caused that dramatic effect when the honeyed voice of the most beautiful woman she had ever seen announced, 'Stay there. I'll come to you.' The woman deftly steered her wheel chair towards their table.

'Hello, Jack. Long time no see. Won't you introduce me to your friend?'

Jack, still in 'having seen a ghost' mode, spluttered, 'Penelope, this is my wife, Margaret. Margaret, Penelope.

Margaret, who completely ignored Penelope, broke the awkward pause which followed the introductions. In an icy sarcastic tone she said to him, 'In case you are wondering why I am here after all these years, well it's just to tell you that I am coming back to you. Mummy and Daddy were killed in a car accident last year in Port Moresby. Maria, the love of my life, has moved on, so there's no real choice for me but to move back with you and continue my crusade to make your life as hellish as you have made mine.'

There was a stunned silence which Penelope broke. 'I think I'll go now. Good night Jack. Margaret.' She nodded briefly in her direction, to be ignored once again.

Penelope left the Club, head held high while fighting the tears stinging her eyes. One last backward glance saw Margaret talking animatedly and Jack, shoulders slumped, silent.

She waited painfully for his explanation of this extraordinary exchange. It came three days' later. He knocked on her door early one morning. She fell into his arms, her heart beat almost palpable. He, in turn, held her tightly for a full minute before setting her down. Their eyes met, hers full of hurt and puzzlement, his tinged with uncharacteristic anger.

'I met Margaret twenty years ago in Port Moresby where she lived with her parents in a mansion at the top end of town. She was quite a stunner, as you can imagine, and spoilt rotten. I was a young Patrol Officer setting out to conquer the world. She had a swathe of ex-pats dancing attendance on her, always keeping her centre stage as a fun-time girl.

'For some reason she singled me out and played me like a fish. I was on patrol a lot, but when I was in town I partied hard. Her mother and father approved of me. I think it was because I had a regular job and wasn't in and out of the dubious activities like the rest of her admirers. I liked Mum and Dad. They were hard working and unpretentious, despite the elaborate life style their only daughter, who was largely uncontrollable, had set up. Anyhow, Margaret was determined that we marry, and what Margaret wanted, Margaret got. So we were.'

'Mum and Dad gave us a house for a wedding present and for a while we were happy. Then cracks started to appear in the marriage. She resented my time away from her, insisting I get a job that kept me at home, but I refused. Being a Patrol Officer was my life.

'Inevitably stories of her affairs reached me and the arguments started, then escalated, as did my drinking. She informed me she was certainly not in the business of breeding so, thankfully, children weren't involved.

'After one particularly fierce exchange on the way home from yet another wild party, I asked her why she had married me. She explained that she was 'running wild' at the time and a gaol sentence was a distinct possibility. Daddy had said he would smooth that over if she promised to settle down. I was livid at having been duped like this. I lost control of the car and life as I knew it. I escaped with a few bruises. She broke her back and both of us descended into our own particular hell.

'Any affection she might have had for me turned to a deep and bitter hatred and all the energy that she had put into being the queen bee of the social set was then directed at making me suffer as much as she did.

'Mum and Dad paid for all the expensive medical treatment and years of rehab but nothing could take away the fact that she was wheelchair bound and would remain so. They were understanding of my position and held no grudge, but were helpless to modify her resolve to bring me to my knees.

'My own guilt was deep and painful too. I did what I could to atone but was never in the race with her bitterness and determination to destroy me. I resolved to just take it. Work became my salvation, which did nothing to improve things. My excessive drinking had come to an abrupt halt. Finally, when I realized I really was at the end of my tether, I plucked up the courage to leave. At the time she was conducting an affair with her carer, the details of which she relayed to me with gusto, knowing the power to hurt in betrayal with a same-sex relationship.

'Mum and Dad were saddened when I announced I was going but they understood my untenable position. They would see that she had the material things she needed and wait for her bitterness to turn to acceptance. Of course, that did not happen – nor ever will.

'I had made enough from investments to live a modest life here where so many ex-pats have come to retire and I have or had carved out some sort of life for myself. But now she has tracked me down and insists we live together as punishment for destroying her life.

'I've survived to date by building a wall around myself that no one can penetrate, wrapping it in humour. I get by. Until you came along and reminded me that life could be different – but not for me. An affair is out of the question. Your reputation would be in tatters in no time, and too much water has gone under the bridge for me to start again with her.

'Oh, Penelope, I am so sorry that we can never get going, because I know we could make a great team, but her venom and my guilt makes that impossible. Thank you for showing me a glimpse of what might have been. That is all I have to live on now. I'd like to think she'd throw me out, but of course she won't, especially now she knows there is someone else around.'

Her tears flowed, as did his.

He held her one more time. 'Please stay vertical and above ground,' he said. He left.

As shattered as she was, she knew that the tears would eventually dry up. They did, allowing her to again take stock of her situation. She would not, could not and should not involve herself with Jack's problem of guilt. That was for him alone to do. What she needed to do was lay down her memories and learn from the experience.

It seemed to her that people came into her life for a reason – to meet a need – and then they left. Or they come for a season when there is much for both to learn. And then, through no fault on her part, they leave. She may have lost the battle for this man but this ending had at least clarified for her what she did and did not want.

Every exciting beginning and tearful ending had led to new learning about herself and the world around her. While it may be that a good man is hard to find, she was equally sure he was somewhere out there for her. For now, she would look for talents she might have and develop these.

With every goodbye you learn. From beginning to end. The Universe sees to that.

WINGS OF FREEDOM

Maurice Hardy

ROB Ford cursed as he thumped his steering wheel – he did not need this. The car's interior lights were fading, confirming the obvious; the battery was flat. Ten minutes earlier he and wife, Michelle, were involved in one of their frequent arguments. This one had been more bitter than usual. It was unresolved when he stormed out. The prospect of returning, apologising and begging her to drive him to work filled him with loathing, but he could see no other option.

He found Michelle in the lounge room. Their two uncooperative daughters were finally ready for school and a stressed Michelle was preparing to leave.

'You have got to be joking. I have to drop the kids off and open the salon by 8.30. Catch the flaming bus.'

'But it's pouring,' pleaded Rob.

'Well there's a fantastic invention called an umbrella. I suggest you use one.'

With briefcase in one hand, umbrella in the other, Rob trudged along the sodden footpath. He was in a foul mood. After covering half the five-hundred metres to the bus stop, he heard a familiar, unwelcome sound. 'The hoon from forty- four,' he muttered.

Since arriving several months ago, this guy had disrupted and infuriated the residents of this previously quiet back street. Usually his burnouts, wheelies and drag-racing activities were confined to the late night and early morning hours. For some unknown reason this morning's wet conditions seemed to have attracted his interest.

The multi-coloured V8 roared past Rob, showering him with road spray. At the end of the street it did two 360-degree spins before the driver gunned the motor for the return journey. After much screeching, sliding and fish tailing the battered sedan regained traction and surged forward.

The driver lost control. Like a charging rhinoceros, the car mounted the kerb, demolished a row of rubbish bins and flattened a street sign, before ploughing head on into an innocent pedestrian. Rob Ford.

For Rob the incident seemed surreal. Time and reality became a blur. First, a sensation of extreme pain, followed by a sound similar to ears popping in a descending plane – only a thousand times more intense.

Next he could feel bones shattering as a sheet of vivid red filled his vision. Somewhere amidst the swirling chaos, Rob was aware of 'floating' above the scene. Police and ambulance officers were examining his crushed body before the tell-tale head shakes confirmed the worst.

'*Shit, am I dead?*' entered Rob's brain, before blackness consumed his all.

ROB awoke in a strange, dark place. A pungent odour invaded his nostrils and the humidity was oppressive. He was coated with slimy goo which contained fragments or shards of glass or egg-like pieces. Confused and disorientated he tried to stand, but discovered a soft ceiling pressing down from above, restricted his movements. As a wave of nausea and tiredness engulfed him, Rob passed out.

When he woke the second time, Rob felt stronger and more alert. In the darkness he was trying to make sense of his predicament when the ceiling lifted. Blinding sunlight flooded in. This forced Rob to close his eyes to escape the glare. When he refocused the scene before him defied belief. His 'soft ceiling' was actually the underside of a huge bird. Recalling nature studies from his school days, Rob studied the imposing creature. With a mainly black head, cream underparts, dark horizontal bars, hooked beak and powerful talons, he was in no doubt – he was looking at a peregrine falcon, a mighty bird of prey – the swiftest of all raptors.

Continuing his observation, Rob discovered he was in a semi conical structure. Tree branches, vines, reeds and grasses had been skilfully bonded and intertwined in its construction, while the floor was carpeted with feathers, animal fur and foliage. To his right he noticed three fluffy, brownish chicks. But something was wrong; these things were gigantic, at least as tall as he. Glancing down at his own form, Rob made a shocking discovery. His body was no longer human but a likeness to his three companions. He was one of them.

Ah I get it, he thought as relief soothed his mind. *I'm having one of those weird dreams where everything is messed up and impossible. Phew, even the accident may be part of this nightmare, thank God.*

Feeling more relaxed Rob studied his new family members. The first barely moved or spoke (squawked), so Rob christened him Dopey. The next he sensed was female. She was chatty, active, busy and alert – Rob named her Twitter. The third was the biggest and strongest and, as Rob discovered, aggressive and bad tempered. Whenever Rob or the others ventured within range they received a barrage of savage pecks; thus the name Pecker seemed apt.

A shadow engulfed the little group accompanied by loud screeching. From the sky a second adult bird arrived carrying a bloodied form in one talon – an unfortunate duck. The original bird (mum) accepted the offering and commenced shredding layers of flesh to share with her eager family. Meanwhile dad, after pausing briefly, extended his broad wings and glided out of sight over the rim of the nest. Although tasteless, Rob found the meal provided an internal feel-good sensation and eased his hunger pains.

Over the ensuing days a similar routine was established. Dad brought a variety of food including a lizard, snake, rabbit, rodents and other birds. Duck, it appeared, was a rare and special treat. Mum too, began spending longer periods away and usually returned with a meal for her appreciative family.

During one of her absences Rob felt his anxiety returning, forcing him to reflect on his situation.

If this is a dream and I'm aware it is a dream, why can't I wake up when I try to? Maybe I've been dosed to the eyeballs with drugs and pain killers after the accident, causing hallucinations... No...This is too vivid, too real and when Pecker pecks it really hurts. Reincarnation...oh shit no... Impossible, there is no such thing...is there? Maybe if I 'die' again I'll return as human. What the hell is going on here?

A solid whack interrupted his thoughts. The side of his head and corner of his left eye erupted with excruciating pain. Pecker was at it again. An angry Rob decided it was time for a counter attack.

Unleashing a flurry of pecks, accompanied by hostile squawks, Rob took his brother by surprise. Pecker backed off in alarm at this unexpected response leaving himself open to more of Rob's precise strikes. Obviously wounded, Pecker retreated and scrambled onto the rim of the nest. However Rob was not finished and continued pursuing his adversary. This bully had to be taught a lesson in life. After several unsuccessful attempts, Rob finally clambered onto the rim. However Pecker was nowhere to be seen.

Rob was unsure what he expected to see as he peered over the edge; maybe a rocky ledge or trees or ground level terrain, but not this. Before him was a sheer drop down an almost vertical cliff face to a rugged valley floor, hundreds of metres below. Totally consumed by acrophobia, he inched his trembling form away from the terrifying void. Returning to the nest, Rob was greeted by agitated cries from both Twitter and Dopey prompting a surge of guilt. A solitary tear rolled down his beak and disappeared into the meshed floor.

Oh my God, I've killed Pecker.

It was a pivotal moment. Rob was forced to accept the truth; this was no dream. A myriad of disturbing thoughts and emotions bombarded his tiny brain as he tried to rationalise and find answers.

This must be a unique, a freak event not supposed to happen. No way should I be aware of my previous existence. If I were to die again, would I remember? Maybe this only happens once...or maybe it's infinite. Am I living straight after my human death, years into the future or, God forbid, in the past?

Loud screeching heralded Mum's return and filled Rob with utter terror.

Oh shit, I've murdered Pecker. Twitter and Dopey will no doubt be able to communicate the events to mum. What is the peregrine justice system? Would I suffer the same fate as my late brother?

Rob was shaking with fear as mum offered him a slice of pigeon. However everything seemed to be playing out as normal. Twitter and Dopey appeared unaffected and if mum did notice Pecker's absence, she gave no indication. Rob couldn't believe it; he had gotten away with murder.

Instinct and nature told Rob this day would eventually arrive. He, and his two siblings, were escorted to the nest edge by mum. From this dizzying height the vast openness of the skies was overpowering and Rob's feeling of acrophobia and vertigo returned with a vengeance. In quick succession Twitter and Dopey plunged from the safety of their home and after a few frantic, awkward flapping manoeuvres achieved their objective – the magic of flight.

Rob had never felt so terrified. He couldn't do it. He dug in with all the strength he could muster; his talons clasped the nest structure and he refused to budge.

'No mum, I don't want to. Please don't make me. There has been a mistake...I'm not really like you, I'm a human being,' he screamed the words in his mind, but the only audible sound to escape was a pathetic squawk. It was futile; mum had no sympathy for cowards. Despite Rob's final desperate efforts to cling on, he was no match for his mother's incredible strength and power. In one swift action he was prised free and nudged into the abyss of nothingness.

Instinct and impulse kicked in and Rob quickly had it mastered. He experimented with different techniques and variations as he soared effortlessly above the valley. Something flashed by. Rob realised it was Twitter, who had apparently decided it was playtime. Moments later Dopey joined in. For hours the trio rose, fell, swooped, dove and soared. Never had Rob known such exhilaration. Never before had he experienced such utter freedom.

IT was a chaotic and desperate scramble to secure a feeding position. Rob was lucky and quickly latching on to a teat, gorged himself with milk. Mother Labrador turned and looked down at her litter approvingly.

THE TRAGEDY OF GARASS AND ASHER

Kasper Beaumont

ASH dragon was moping. Of all the shifters in Flame Mountain, he had the misfortune to be in love with the same one as his best friend, Garass Black. He snorted with frustration, and a plume of smoke billowed from his nostrils. Extending his large grey wings as far as they would go, he resembled a strange giant bird, perching on the very edge of the expansive volcanic crater of Flame Mountain. The emerald scales on the undersides of his wings glistened in the sunlight, as far below him, molten lava bubbled away, its searing heat enveloping him.

The seventeen-year old closed his eyes firmly in an attempt to purge the image of Larissa Black from his head. Sadly this did the opposite, by reliving the vision of two days ago, when she smiled at him. He had fallen head over heels in love for the very first time. Unable to eat or sleep, he was too scared to fly in case he blindly flew into a mountain, for her image filled his every waking thought.

He recalled the fateful morning when he had seen her sitting, brushing her long hair by the Blue Crater Lake, halfway down the volcano-side. Distracted, whilst glancing her way, he had tripped over his own two feet. His younger sisters who were helping to braid Larissa's black locks, noticed their clumsy brother's misfortune, and giggled together. Larissa turned briefly in his direction and they exchanged heat-filled glances. He had looked away quickly, but not soon enough, for the damage had been done. Now he was madly in love.

But I can't love Larissa, frustrated Ash thought for the umpteenth time, scratching his claws against the side of the crater. *My best friend Garass has been deeply in love with her for two years, so there be no way I'd ever betray his friendship by chasing his girl. Plus she's a black and I'm a grey. Sure that's no impossible barrier to us being together, but she'd be much better off within her own clan. No ... I just need to ride out these feelings until they pass and we can all remain friends. Yes, that's for the best,* he finally decided.

Glad to settle his thoughts, the young dragon shifted his weight forward, preparing to launch into the sky, when someone landed on him from above, and both tumbled down the mountainside. Ash finally managed to catch his claws on an outcropping to stop their descent. A landslide of rocks rained down beneath them, scaring away a herd of scrawny mountain goats.

'Are you crazy?' he shouted angrily, but turning his head, his anger melted away in an instant. Clinging to Ash desperately was a graceful black dragon, slightly larger than himself, with luminous black eyes showing concern at his anger. Larissa.

'Oh, I'm really sorry Ash, I just meant to surprise you, but flew in too fast. Can you forgive me?'

'Ah! There be nothing to forgive, you clumsy bird-brain,' he replied tenderly. 'I'm glad you weren't coming the other way, or we'd have fallen into the lava. Then I would be cranky. No harm done, I guess. Are you alright?'

She grimaced. 'Yes, apart from whacking my neck hard on the way down. I'll shift and see if it feels better. It's a long neck to have aching, to be sure.'

The two dragon forms shimmered on the mountainside, replaced by two leather-clad people. Asher was a rugged-looking young man with spiky black hair and a little stubble on his chin. To him Larissa looked like a goddess with her beautiful hair woven in intricate braids emphasising large black eyes. His eyes were drawn to her full pink lips and he felt his mouth go dry as he quickly looked away.

'Can you give it a rub for me?' Larissa asked, unaware of the overwhelming youthful urges soaring through her friend. When Ash still didn't turn around she grabbed him by the shoulder and spun him. 'Please, Ash. Surely you're not mad with me over an accident.'

Larissa looked hard at Asher, who seemed unable to speak. His yellow-green eyes glowed with emotion, his lips trembled and every muscle in his body seemed tense.

Misinterpreting his lust for fear, she laughed it off, 'Don't worry. I won't tell Garass you touched me. He is a bit possessive sometimes and I don't want to spoil your friendship. I know you're like brothers.' She gave him a reassuring pat on the back. Asher's heart raced and butterflies swirled uncomfortably in his abdomen.

Rubbing sweaty palms on his leather pants did little good and he inwardly chastised himself for being unable to think of a light-hearted reply.

'OK, sit down and I'll rub your sore neck,' he finally managed. *At least she'll be looking the other way and won't see the desire in my face.*

Larissa sat on the flattest place she could find on the mountain. Removing her black leather jacket caused Asher's heart to skip a beat. Underneath she wore a white cotton blouse, which clung to her damp skin in the heat of the volcano. He could clearly see her perky brown nipples and full breasts tantalisingly within reach.

Giving a sigh to steady his racing heart, Asher moved her heavy braids so he could see her neck. 'Where does it hurt?' he asked, concern in his voice.

'Well it feels like it goes all the way up into my brain,' she replied a little grumpily. 'If you can rub my shoulders first, I'll undo the braids so you can rub right up into my hair. Thank-you so much for assisting me. I feel like such a clumsy dragon around you sometimes.'

Asher was giving long stroking rubs along her shoulder blades and paused as her words sank in. Intrigued, he asked, 'Why would you be clumsy around me? We hang out together heaps with Garass and his gang.'

Larissa flushed to a deep red as she struggled with the complicated braids. Noticing this, Asher took her hair out of her hands and worked to un-weave them for her. She still did not answer his question and when he leant over to try and gauge her expression, she turned away. 'Have I done something wrong?' he asked, confused as to her avoidance. 'We're still friends, right?'

She nodded and he felt relieved, although still puzzled by her silence. He finished untying her braids and her long black hair fell in waves to the rocks around her. Caressing it gently, he admired the beautiful sheen from fragrant oils she used, before pushing it over her shoulders so he could rub her neck. As he started massaging up her neck and into her hair, she gave a low moan and hugged her knees to her chest, with hair spilling over her bent face.

Asher had never experienced anything more sensual and pleasurable than this physical contact, with the young woman who filled his dreams and every waking moment. His body responded to her gentle moans in ways he had never experienced, and involuntarily a small moan escaped his own lips.

Her body tensed and she breathlessly whispered, 'Oh, Asher! You don't know how long I've waited for you to touch me.'

Taking him by surprise, Larissa turned suddenly and pinned him to the ground, her body on top of his and her hair surrounding their faces like a black curtain. Her lips were on his, kissing him passionately, her tongue exploring his mouth and her hands racing down to grip his hips firmly. In the heat of passion, they lost themselves in each other's arms.

Finding it hard to concentrate with the rush of desire, Asher rolled to the side and pushed her away gently. 'Larissa, I'm sorry, but I think we need to stop. If Garass ever found out I'd kissed you, there'd be hell to pay.'

'I don't care,' she insisted. 'Yes, I know I'll probably marry him, but why can't I just do this, just this once. I've wanted you for so long and I finally see it in your eyes too. Surely once won't hurt and we'd both be happier afterwards that we had this one chance together. Please Asher, I promise I'll never tell a soul.'

Poor Asher was torn between raging hormones and his sense of duty to his best friend. *Could they embrace once and never again?* Would that be enough, or would it start a fire that would burn them up and consume their families and friends in a path of destruction? Asher knew he would never be able to look at Garass with a clear conscience again and all for a fleeting moment of forbidden love with this beautiful woman.

His thoughts were interrupted by the sight of Larissa pulling her thin blouse over her head and tossing it on the ground. All arguments were forgotten now at the sight of her full breasts and he instinctively reached for them. She reclined backwards against the rocky soil and he quickly rolled her jacket to place it under her head for a pillow, all the while admiring her beauty. He caressed her firm breasts, teasing her nipples with an eager tongue.

Moaning with pleasure, Asher's skin was on fire with her hands exploring his chest and feverishly prying off his leather vest. Locking her lips passionately on his, Larissa's nimble fingers explored his biceps, chest, well-defined abdominal muscles and his straining leather pants.

Asher tried to reciprocate, but could not seem to draw his hands away from her bosom, noting the gentle touches seemed to elicit even more pleasure than the firm ones. Pulling the aroused young man on top of her once more, she gripped his leather-clad hips firmly, guiding him, and his body responded to the rhythm as they moved in unison.

Flapping wings gave them but a split-second warning before sharp claws reached down to drag Asher off the girl. A black dragon screeched with rage, flying high in the air before throwing him down to certain death in the lowlands.

It was fortunate Asher was a faster shape-shifter than most. He managed to transform himself and flew upwards a split second before he would have crashed to his death on the sharp rocks. Ignoring the pain of his torn flesh, he soared upwards to meet the wrath of Garass, who was turning towards Larissa.

The black dragon was larger than Ash, as black as night with ebony scales that glittered in the sunlight, but the smaller grey was spurred on by a desire to protect Larissa. Beating his wings in hot pursuit of his former best friend, he pleaded, 'Garass, wait! It's my fault, not Larissa's, please let me explain. Please, you know I think of you as a brother.'

'I will not hear you, traitor,' growled Garass. 'You have stolen my most prized possession and I will kill you for it if it's the last thing I do. Pleading to be treated as a brother will not save you from your fate.'

While speaking angrily, Garass had his back to Ash, but the younger dragon was too scared to make the first strike. He watched Garass check on Larissa as she sat crying on the crater's edge, holding her blouse across her chest. Then the black turned to strike.

Ash steeled himself for the onslaught of fire and claws that came at him like a storm. He was turned about in the wild air currents as flames raged around him. Garass mercilessly tore a huge gash across his back, the flames searing his tender insides.

Ash screeched in agony, but steadied himself with strong wing beats. As Garass paused to rekindle his fiery breath, Ash struck.

Flying in underneath his opponent, he raked his claws along Garass' belly and bit off the end of his tail, which dropped like a rock to the ground far below.

The black roared in fury and flew directly into Ash, causing one wing to fold back painfully with an audible snap. The grey screeched in pain and hurled a fire ball into Garass' face, momentarily blinding him. Ash flapped with one maimed wing. Flying in for another brutal assault, Garass crashed into Ash again. Unfortunately this manoeuvre backfired on Garass and sent him spinning out of control with a broken leg. His uncontrolled trajectory took him straight to where his girlfriend was standing on the edge of the crater, pleading with them both to stop fighting.

The plummeting dragon barely had time to glance at the terrified face of Larissa, before he ploughed into her, and they fell directly into the boiling lava of Flame Mountain.

With one wing hanging limp, Ash looked on with horror. Wide eyed, he gasped and flew erratically over to the crater. To his dismay, he saw only the bubbling lava below, with no sign of either Garass or their beloved Larissa.

With a stabbing pain in his chest, Ash collapsed to the volcano's rim in shock. *How could they have vanished without a trace?* Not Larissa, the first girl he had ever loved. *My beautiful Larissa,* with a smile just for him and long dark hair flowing like a river. The shock was just too much for him to bear and he wept painful crystal tears into the volcano, watching them disintegrate as they fell into the steaming crater.

A disturbance in the lava lake distracted him from his thoughts when a large blob covered in dripping red lava shot out of the crater straight towards him. 'What the …?'

He was bowled over backwards by a furious and vengeful Garass who tore at him with sharp claws and words, 'How could you? My Larissa. You killed her, you killed her. This is entirely your fault. You betrayer!'

Stung by the blows and words, Ash barely lifted a claw against the attack, but Garass too, seemed emotionally spent and collapsed into a ball, shaking in rage and grief.

Trying to console his friend, Ash placed his good wing over Garass. 'I'm so sorry my friend, I never meant for these things to happen. It's all a terrible tragedy. I am so sorry she's dead. I … I can't believe she's gone. She was such a wonderful dragon.' Crystal tears came again as he tried to console the black dragon.

Garass growled and rasped one last remark. 'I will never forgive you for this Asher Grey. You may live a hundred years, but this will haunt you every day of them. Be gone from here and never let me see you again.'

The black pushed him roughly down the mountainside and Ash let himself fall, shifting into human form again as he tumbled over and over to the foothills below.

When he finally reached the bottom, the shirtless mountain man was covered in scratches and bruises from head to foot, but the thing that hurt the most was his broken heart.

He crawled on hands and knees back to his home cave, but there would be no sunshine in his life for a great many years to come, as his heart hardened to love and friendship.

WINDS OF CHANGE
Santina Cardillo

The air, it is so crisp and clear,
A script of new beginnings written in the wind,
From the highest tip of the Himalayas to the red dust downunder.
Clear your minds, shut your eyes, you will hear it like a clap of thunder.

Faces new and old you'll see,
Silhouetted against the setting sun.
A new age dawning, no longer opaque.
Clear your minds open your eyes – you will see everything laid at your feet.

The warmth is like liquid gold,
The heat so intense it reaches right into your very soul.
You have never felt so complete, unconditionally loved, magnificent and at
peace.
Clear you minds, open your heart - you will never ever want to leave.

All around you'll feel the serenity.
Will-o'-the-Wisps find their way.
Heaven welcomes, to never ever let them stray.
Clear your minds, feel the Fae - they have been with you all the way.

Energy and stillness both abound
No need to never ever frown,
Every moment a gift of clarity.
Clear your minds, remember the past has passed, live for now and be
the director, producer and the cast.

Never ever to feel afraid, unloved or shunned,
Never ever to feel small, too tall, or not the mold.
Never ever to feel not tough enough, smart enough, giving enough, pretty
enough.
 ENOUGH!
Clear your minds, still your heart, forgive yourself; you are perfect *exactly* as
you are.

THE DIAMOND KEY

Kelly Brettell

MAGGIE remembers hearing, probably on *Dr Phil* or *Oprah* that your first memories define your life. If that was true her life would have been defined by death, but it was not. For years she was never sure which memory came first; the Vegemite sandwich memory or her father and the dirt street memory.

She was never sure who the little blonde boy sitting next to her in the Vegemite sandwich memory was. Over time, as she pieced her life together, she realised it was Finn not Marshall, because at that time Finn was still alive and Marshall was not yet born.

In the memory, she is sitting in front of a window, on a kitchen bench with a little blonde boy; Finn as it turns out, and they are eating Vegemite sandwiches. Their mother and grandmother are standing in front of them, ready to catch them if they fall. Their mother says a teary good-bye and Maggie and Finn continue eating their sandwiches, blissfully unaware of the drama in their lives. How could they be?

Their father has taken an overdose and is in a coma fighting for his life. Something in his outwardly happy life with a young wife, two small children and an emerging career is not what it seems.

Two days before, Maggie and Finn had been strapped into their booster seats while their mother drove, frantically trying to reach the hospital in time, but trying also to keep their father's actions private. Their father collapsed into a coma as their mother turned into the hospital where she and Finn had been born.

Lives were shattered and questions never answered. Their father would not talk about his actions. When the police interviewed him and when their mother asked 'why?' he simply said he could not remember.

Their mother tried, but could not understand her husband's actions. She spent her life convincing herself their world was solid and their family perfect. People knew, but no-one spoke of it, so it became a secret and no-one ever told the children. Maggie realised later there had been hints, such as when Marshall accidently took a sleeping tablet instead of a headache tablet and their aunty commented, 'another Fitzpatrick sick of living'. It made no sense to her at the time, and she was accustomed to ignoring their Auntie's caustic remarks. She put it out of her mind until the day she learnt the truth.

Maggie was relieved her father was still alive when she learnt the truth. He remained unaware she knew his secret, but she felt closer to him knowing. As a child she had been told the story many times by her strict Catholic grandparents who always left out the cause of their son's hospitalisation. Her father was an only child and his actions would have almost destroyed them. They told her their version of her father's fight for his life. How his best friend, a doctor, had told them to prepare to lose their son and how a vial of Lourdes water was placed under his pillow. According to family folklore, they had experienced a miracle and had their faith to thank for it, as well as a cheeky nurse who tapped her father on the backside saying 'Time to wake-up Mr Fitzpatrick'. Maggie believed this whole heartedly; so much so, she took Bernadette as her confirmation name, after Saint Bernadette of Lourdes.

She wished she had known the truth while her grandparents were still alive. She may have understood them better. Her grandparents had told her their version of the story because she did not know the truth. They could retain their pride in their son and their confidence in themselves without fear of a knowing look or judgement. They could tell Maggie the way they wished it had been and allow themselves to almost believe it.

In her second memory Maggie is in her father's arms. He is running down a dirt street. The dirt is red and dry. He is running so fast she can feel the wind hit her face and his heart pounding against her chest. She knows there is a sense of urgency. What she does not know is her brother Finn is dead.

After her father's suicide attempt, the family had literally run away and were living and working in a remote Indigenous community. On the day of the dirt street memory, Maggie and Finn had been playing at the end of their street with a boy named Adam. Adam had not let Finn play and she had not stood up for him either. Left out of the game, Finn had gone home. Her mother gave him a peanut and picked him up, accidently brushing a sore on his leg. Finn cried out in pain and inhaled the nut, blocking his airways. Her mother ran with Finn to the hospital, staffed by two nurses, friends of her parents. Her father was alerted and he came for her. The Flying Doctor was called, but Finn died.

Maggie's parents never told people the real version of Finn's death. The grief was enough to deal with, without judgement. Her mother illogically hated the name Adam afterward. Her father, who had once tried to take his own life, was strong enough to keep living. Her parents did not blame her, her father did not blame her mother, but Maggie blamed them. She asked them again and again why they let her brother die. These were the words of a child though; as an adult she knew her parents had not let Finn die. He should not have died but he did.

Maggie was four when Finn died, and younger; she is not sure how much younger, when her father tried to die. They are her first memories. They play out in her mind like dreams, but as much as she wishes they were dreams, they are memories. They are her first and defining memories through which she learnt about death and loss. She also learnt things are not always as they seem, people are not always honest and their judgements can be harsh. She later learnt lightning can strike twice.

Maggie grew up without all this knowledge, but with memories and gaps left by unanswered questions. She grew up with a feeling; more than a feeling, a certainty there were family secrets, things you did not talk about. She remembers her mother's anger at her talking to a friend about Finn, accusing her of gaining attention through her brother's death. She knew she was not to talk about Finn but she did not understand why. Later, when Marshall died from cancer she refused to allow him to become another secret and for a while she silently asked the same question 'why did you let him die?' She did not ask it of her parents. There was desperation and denial in the way they tried to stop Marshall from dying. She asked the question of his wife and doctors, but in time she realised no-one let him die. Marshall should not have died either. He was too young and too loved to die, but he did.

Maggie was a wife and mother herself when she learnt her father's coma had been a suicide attempt, and how hers and her mother's actions had contributed to Finn's death. For a while it made her question her life, because it was not what she thought it was. She questioned herself, because how had she been so easily deceived? She did not blame her parents for keeping secrets. They were coping with their own worlds being shattered. She could not imagine how they lived through the night Finn died, let alone the rest. She was shaken to the core and thought she would never trust the world again, but she did.

Maggie's first happy memory had been the diamond key. It was like Santa Claus, the Easter Bunny and the Tooth Fairy all wrapped up in one. She found the key in the back yard of one of their many homes. The key was printed with the word 'diamond' so she thought it was a key to diamonds.

She believed one day she would find a treasure chest full of diamonds and her key would fit the lock.

The diamond key gave her hope and allowed her to dream. In reality 'Diamond' was the brand but she did not know that at the time. She saw the word 'diamond' and saw wonder, mystery and treasure and no-one disillusioned her. They allowed her to dream.

Maggie's final memory, as she closes her eyes for the last time is not death. She realises those first memories had not defined her life. Her last memory is the diamonds and the treasures in her life. Her brothers she had held tightly within her heart, her parents who had found the strength to live for their daughters but were now at rest with their sons; her sister who she and Marshall had shared their childhood with and whom she had grown old with; Marshall's daughter, her niece, who had bought joy to broken hearts; the man she had loved and never lost; the children she had kept safe, and their children; all looking at her with diamonds in their eyes.

The diamond key is the memory that has defined her life. The hope and the wonder it brought when she needed to dream. Maggie's first memory of promised treasures and her last memory of her life's treasures blend together as she closes her eyes for the final time.

I LOVE HER JEWEL-SEA

Tatiana Werle-Bertling

'LOOK! Look over there, Daddy! Quickly, you'll miss out Daddy!' The little girl was bouncing up and down in a flurry of excitement that immediately drew the tourists' attention. My grin widened as my gaze followed the girl's and I spotted the silver-grey figures slipping through the water. My oma and papa's cameras joined the tourists' chorus of clicks as the dolphins came into full sight. The dolphins leapt and flipped around the slow monohull a couple of times before discovering a current and vanishing from sight. The little display was all over in a couple of minutes and half the boat had missed it. Yet, it was moments like these that made the ocean and life itself so magically alluring. A contented sigh escaped my lips as I closed my eyes to better feel the sun falling like a warm curtain on my bare shoulders, the ocean breeze playfully fingering my sun-bleached hair, and the salt spray's revitalising sting on my arms and legs.

More tourists filtered out in the hope of seeing dolphins, making the aft deck uncomfortably crowded. I nudged Papa as a way of grabbing his attention and walked through the large air-conditioned room that took up two-thirds of the deck towards the fore while my oma went to the second – and middle – deck to keep an eye on our bags while she relaxed. We found the fore deck already occupied by five or six bikinis sprawled carelessly across the deck and convenient benches. I chose a spot on a bench where I could lean lazily over the railing and watch the sun dance over the waves, causing them to shimmer and glint so brightly that it hurt to look. Yet it was so stunningly that it hurt not to!

Papa ruined the moment by switching from cool dad to daggy dad when he followed an urge to do his *Titanic* impression in the prow of the ship. I simply groaned and looked the other way, relishing the tangy ocean-scent in my nostrils and the warmth of the sun covering me like a blanket all the way from my shoulders to my toes.

My papa attempted to convince me to apply sunscreen, to no avail. He might have been a pale Pom, vulnerable to the sun's rays;

but I was Aussie born and bred, and as we were only just beginning to come into mid-Summer, would only tan spectacularly (and it was so, as I had many compliments on the golden-brown hue of my skin upon returning home).

How long I sat there, soaking up vitamin-D and dozing between intermittent snatches of conversation, I'll never know. It ended abruptly when the tour guide announced over the ship's loudspeakers that we were nearing the first spot in the Great Barrier Reef that we were to explore. This announcement jolted the last shred of laziness from me and I was an eager participant of the excited buzz that spread through the ship like wildfire. I raced Papa up the stairs to the middle deck where Oma was waiting, camera in hand. I sighed tolerantly – nearly half a century Down Under and she was still acting like a tourist.

About twenty happy-snaps later, we set off to find the wetsuit racks. One of the crewmen assisted me in selecting a wetsuit roughly my size before I wambled over to several brightly-coloured buckets filled with water, and fished out a snorkel-mask with some fins. Upon returning to the middle deck Oma insisted we try on our new 'outfits' for photos. Apparently her SD card had limitless memory.

I struggled a bit slipping the wetsuit over my togs as both were slightly damp from ocean-spray, but managed eventually. The wetsuit felt cold and spongy, and fairly rough too – so that it had the same effect on my spine as nails dragged along a blackboard. I must confess that I have never felt fatter than when standing for photos in that pudgy wetsuit a couple of sizes too big. Next came the mask and fins. I ended up having to tie my unruly hair into a ponytail in a desperate attempt to prevent (or at least minimise) the mask's rubber-strap tearing it out.

The boat slowed to a halt and we leapt downstairs, racing to be the first in the water. It was difficult walking across the deck as, only being a monohull, its rocking was more pronounced at rest than that of a catamaran. The crew undid the chains that blocked the gaps in the railing of the bottom deck and tourists poured from the ship like froth from a bottle. I laughed out loud, thoroughly enjoying the atmosphere, and dove in.

Below the surface, a whole new world greeted my sight: schools of fish of every size, colour, and species flitted like so many flocks of birds around palaces of coral just as diverse. Brightly-coloured anemones bloomed from unexpected nooks, crannies and crevasses; and the sun glinted off sedimentary particles spinning in the grip of mini-currents, lending that little touch of magic to the overall scene. My breath rasped funnily in the plastic-snorkel and the world was slightly distorted through my mask. I tested my fins with the flick of an ankle and was delighted at how far, fast, and easily I was propelled through the water. My oma swam off in her own direction almost immediately, leaving my papa and me to explore together. We swam a little-way out in order to have a bit of peace and solitude from the tourist-mob while we snorkelled.

Almost immediately, a school of colourful parrot-fish playing around a pink turret of Staghorn coral captivated my attention. I floated, mesmerised by the sight for about five-minutes until Papa grabbed my attention by swimming below me and waving. He surfaced for a breath before kicking-out strongly towards the seabed, where a giant clam nestled between two coral-stacks, mouth wide-open. He swam right up to it and touched it, causing it to hastily snap shut. He allowed the ocean's pressure to carry him back up to the surface where he blew the water from his snorkel. He looked so much like a whale that I clapped and back-flipped. What? It was funny, alright?

I absolutely adored the way water made bumbling, klutzy me seem so graceful – I was definitely going to take advantage at every opportunity! We swam around for ages (there's no conceivable way that I could possibly tell how long) just admiring the diversity of life in the ocean-environ we were immersed in.

Looking back now, thinking of the beauty and variety offered by the crystal waters of the Pacific, I cannot help but think of a line from my all-time favourite poem: *I love her jewel-sea* and realise how true that really is.

THE BIRD IN THE HAND

Belinda Janz

WHEN Jim was made redundant from his job, Liz worried about how they would manage financially. She also wondered if he would be able to get another job easily, given his age. Jim however took it in his stride. He promptly announced it was time to retire and that they should go travelling.

'How will we manage?' Liz asked, thinking long term.

Jim tried to reassure her they had enough money tucked away in their rainy-day fund to enjoy a good holiday. Neither had travelled far over the years though they had talked about what they would like to see when Jim retired. He had always made the big decisions for them. If he thought they would be fine, then that was that, Liz conceded.

On Saturday, Jim noticed in the newspaper an advertisement for volunteers to monitor and study the Swift Parrots on Maria Island, off the east coast of Tasmania. Preference would be given to couples who would be available for an eight-month period from September to the end of April.

'That is us Lizzie,' Jim promptly announced. Over the next week had set about researching what the job entailed, where they would live and how to get there, should they be accepted. There was never any doubt in his mind. They would get the job.

From Jim's interest in bird watching, he knew the Swift Parrot was on the endangered list. The outcome of a study, some time back, showed there were only about one thousand pairs left in the wild with the population declining. Eighteen sites had been established as important for the species in New South Wales, Victoria and Tasmania.

The breeding season in the Tasmanian area was between September and December. Around March and April the birds would begin migrating back to south-eastern mainland Australia. It had been loosely suggested the declining numbers could come down to a dilemma with an Alpha/Omega problem. Liz knew right away what that meant. Jim was very much the Alpha male in their relationship and as such she had taken on a more subordinate role when she was younger. As she was getting older though, she was beginning to question just how much she had given up on what she would have liked to have done over the years.

Accommodation and transport to the island would be provided for the successful applicants.

Liz could tell Jim was really keen on doing this more than just for a holiday. Liz was less enthusiastic thinking she knew nothing about these birds – not even what they looked like.

Jim set about finding pictures and information to show her, all the while speaking as if they were already a chosen couple. Three couples were required for the Maria Island study. This offered each couple a six-hour morning shift followed the next day by a six-hour afternoon shift and then a day off on a rotating roster. Jim sent off their application hoping they would be accepted. Liz secretly hoped they would not. While a holiday sounded nice, the thought of a strings-attached adventure, as Jim called it, was not that appealing, especially in such a remote place.

A phone call a week and a half later confirmed they were indeed one of the chosen couples to start the study in six weeks. One of their sons and his family were going to move into their home while they were away.

The weeks passed quickly till only the last minute things had to be sorted. Then it was time for the goodbyes to friends and family.

The flight to Hobart had been fine but the ferry-crossing the next day from Triabunna to the jetty area in the Darlington Bay of Maria Island was rough. Liz and Jim had been glad to go ashore.

They were met by the two Rangers, Athol and Roy, who lived on the Island. They explained their accommodation blocks had not arrived yet on the island due to recent rough weather.

For now they were going to be staying with the other two couples, who arrived the day before, in the Darlington Penitentiary building. This had been once a place of internment.

Today it was a basic accommodation block with bunk-bed rooms. Normally nothing was supplied except mattress, a table, some chairs and a wood heater. But for the three couples, linen had been added to six bunk beds and towels provided.

As they walked towards the Penitentiary building, one of the rangers pointed out the toilet and hot-water shower block and barbecue area. There was no electricity nor running water at the Penitentiary building but a portable light tower had been provided by the rangers. They could use the barbecues as they liked but, as no kitchen equipment was supplied, they would be allowed up to the rangers' headquarters and accommodation block to cook and do laundry.

Inside their temporary sleeping building, Jim and Liz met Louisa, Tom, Roz and Tim – their working partners for the study ahead. They too were retirees and had met each other while traveling around north Queensland on their Grey-Nomad travels.

After Athol gave a brief history of the Penitentiary building, they all walked across to the rangers' station. As they walked, Athol pointed to a large space that had been set aside for three converted shipping containers to be set up for their temporary accommodation. A small food allowance came with the job. They could organize supplies through the rangers and they would be delivered to the island.

Liz soon realized she was the only one who was hesitant about the whole experience.

Everything was so basic, even the transport which turned out to be bicycles. Liz would rather walk because she had not been on a bike since school. It was all a bit overwhelming for her so she decided to go for a walk back to the jetty. A couple of backpackers had also caught the ferry over to the island but they were lucky to be only staying three days and then they could move on. *Not us, we are here for eight months*, sighed Liz.

As she sat on the warm jetty boards, she became aware of someone moving around behind her. Looking around from left to right didn't reveal anyone so she got up and walked up towards the trees on the way to the visitor's centre. A dark figure of a man was moving in and out of the trees. He seemed to have his arms stretched up to the trees at times as if he was reaching for something but Liz could not see what he had in his hands. Liz decided to walk in the trees too, to see what the man was trying to reach, maybe she would be able to reach it for him.

She called out 'Hello. Is there anyone there?'

She felt instantly silly. Of course someone was there – she had just seen him.

As Liz stepped out of the trees again to the path, she heard a high-pitched chattering noise start up on the other side of the trees. She walked back in and looked around to see where the noise was coming from. As she walked through the trees, the noise stopped. She was startled to see the mysterious man again, coming slowly towards her.

How had he got back to this side of the trees so quickly? thought Liz. 'Hello,' she said smiling at the man as he approached with his head down as if focusing on what he carried in his cupped hands. Liz looked at his hands too and there sat a beautiful coloured bird. It was mostly green with a blue crown and a little dab of red, like rouge on its face. Liz recognized it from photos Jim had shown her as one of the rare Swift Parrots.

With the man now only a few steps away, she decided to introduce herself. 'Hello, I am Liz and I am here to study these little birds. My husband tells me they are rare and on the endangered list.'

'I am René Maugé, my Lady,' he replied as he stretched out his cupped hands as if to hand the bird to her. Liz did not hesitate, for in that moment it was as if she was under a spell, dazzled by the bird's beauty and amazed at how it was quite content to just sit there in the man's hands. She reached out and allowed the bird to be transferred gently into her own cupped hands. The bird looked up at her and she could have sworn it winked at her.

'How silly, birds do not wink – do they?' She asked the question half aloud looking up, expecting to hear the man's answer but he had disappeared. How strange. He was just here and now he has disappeared as if he vanished into thin air.

Liz walked back through the trees to the Visitors' Centre. The bird just sat comfortably in her hands not frightened even when she walked up the stairs. The young lady volunteering at the visitor's centre was on the veranda putting up new notices on the board.

She turned as Liz reached the top step. 'Wow what a beauty,' she said softly so as to not frighten the bird.

'Yes a man called René Maugé handed him to me just now in the trees over there.' I used my chin to indicate which trees I meant.

'You do realize', the volunteer said, 'that these little guys are a protected species. You had best not let the rangers catch you with this little feller.'

'Oh I am Liz, one of the new volunteer recruits, over here for eight months to study the Swift Parrot and to see if we can determine why they are declining in numbers.'

'Nice to meet you Liz, I am Jodie. I live on the mainland and come across to help out here at the visitor's centre once a week during the Spring and Summer when we have the bulk of our tourists.

'I had best put this little one back in the trees; like you said they are endangered and I do not want to cause them any trouble. I will no doubt see you around over the next eight months,' Liz said.

Liz walked off towards the trees with her new little friend, but Jodie recalled her, asking if she really had been given the bird by René Maugé. 'Surely not *the* René Maugé; he was a French zoologist who died in eighteen hundred and two and is buried at Point Maugé. You must have heard a similar name, surely."

After her experience of meeting face to face with one of the Swift Parrots, Liz had found the adventure had been enjoyable. She wanted to find out more about the Frenchman. Maybe the ranger would know.

She hurried back to tell Jim the good news that some of the parrots had arrived early to the island and about meeting René Maugé; maybe he would be able to help them too.

METAMORPHOSIS
Santina Cardillo

There upon the molten rock,
Liquid gold and ruby hot,
Transcending emotion from the core;
A spewing eruption set to shock,
A travesty of fiery rage, shooting through the layers' crack.
Stone upon stone, ashes upon ashes,
A new age dawning, in this we trust.

There within the funnel's eye,
Almighty power does there reside.
A petulant child tilting and swaying,
Destruction, devastation his only path.
Lives upon lives, dust upon dust,
A new age dawning, this is a must.

There above the oceans wide,
The silent enemy starts to creep:
A trickle to a torrent in a heartbeat.
Ancient graves long buried, rise up again,
No stone unturned, nowhere to flee
Skin upon skin, grief upon grief,
A new age dawning, a new belief.

___oOo___

There below the deep abyss,
She awakes and shakes, with a hiss.
All scatters and shatters high above,
The screams, the suffering, the silence before the aftershock,
Crumbling dreams forever lost.
Trees upon trees, pain upon pain,
A new age dawning, there is nothing left to gain.

There upon the molten rock,

Within the funnel's eye, there is a changing tide.

There above the ocean wide,

Below the deep abyss, there is a changing tide.

What once was, is no longer more.

Joy upon joy, peace upon peace,

A new age dawning, we will release.

EROMANGA'S BREAK: GO TO WOE

R. William Penshorn

EVERYONE called him Eromanga. No one really knew his proper name. He had almost forgotten it himself. He never ever learned to read or write nevertheless he was quite smart, most of the time anyway. He was tough and ruggedly handsome, somewhere in the later part of his fifties. He never knew his birth date. He lived in a little hut on a sheep station somewhere about one hundred kilometres west of a small outback town. A four-strand barbed wire fence with a small swinging gate surrounded the hut.

Eromanga made his living by checking paddock and boundary fences. Trapping dingoes earned him extra money as he collected a bounty for their scalps. He had seven trained hunting dogs, four of which were bitches. There was not a pure bred among them but they all knew their job and were good at it. He treated them all like family. Each answered to its own name. There were Ray Ray, Sissy, Pal, Ricki, Bear, Tuppy and Louie. They all loved their master and he loved them too, especially Ray Ray. He was a magnificent specimen, half Collie and half German Shepherd. He was Eromanga's favourite. A woman had shared Eromanga's life, years before. It was good while it lasted but the loneliness got at her and she took to the drink. It was her downfall.

Jackson Tully, the station manager, supplied Eromanga with an ex-army Jeep. He worked hard at his job. Every once in a while he got a bit of cash in his kitty. With the management's blessing, he would drive into town for a week or two and spend it all on 'wine, women and song', not to mention a touch of gambling. 'I'd always blow the rest,' he would chuckle.

When in town, he would always stay at a pub, the Royal Hotel, where he would hand over his loot to Al, the publican, and ask him to let him know when the money ran out. He always left his dogs at the hut where there were nearby bore drains for water and plenty of wildlife for them to fend for themselves. Eromanga got along well with the regular patrons at the Royal and often bragged about his beloved dogs.

147

One afternoon Eromanga reached in under his bed and pulled out an old biscuit tin, opened it and counted a wad of cash. He grinned to himself and said, 'I think it's time I took meself for another break.' It was not uncommon for him to talk to himself.

He took the biscuit tin and placed it under the passenger seat of the Jeep. He took a shower under a bucket pulley set-up attached to a branch of a nearby tree. He went to the hut, put on his best trousers, a pair of riding boots and his cleanest dirty-shirt, packed a bit of gear into an old port, left the hut and closed the door.

He gave his hounds a friendly pat. He started the motor to head to town. The dogs seemed to sense he was leaving. They jumped and barked until the Jeep was out of sight. It was a slow moving gravel road most of the way.

Within three hours Eromanga pulled the Jeep up in front of the Royal Hotel. He grabbed hold of his port and biscuit tin and entered the place. About twenty regular drinkers were in the bar room, mainly men. A few played pool on a full-size billiard table at the far end. Juke Box music played Slim Dusty's *The Biggest Disappointment in the Family was Me* in the background.

A pretty dimple-faced blonde served behind the bar. With her was an overweight balding man, smartly dressed in a shirt, tie, paisley vest, striped trousers and polished shoes. 'Well look what the wind blew in, Di,' he said, 'How are you doin' Eromanga? Back for a bit more punishment are ya?'

'Call it punishment if you like Al. Let's just say I'm here for a bit more of the usual.' Eromanga gave a small chuckle. Most of the regulars watching joined in with a chuckle or two. Eromanga placed the biscuit tin on the bar and opened it.

Al, the bar man, gawked at the contents then gave Di a wink. She smiled and showed her distinctive dimples. 'You can have room 5,' Al said. 'It opens to the front veranda. You know where it is.'

'Right next to me,' said Di. 'I'm in Room 4.' Eromanga gave her a grin.

'Give me a big coldy before I go up, Al. I'm as thirsty as ten camels on the wrong side of the Simpson Desert.'

'Sure Eromanga,' said Al, 'first one's on the house. Ha ha ha.'

Al handed a glass to Eromanga and went to place the biscuit tin below the counter. 'Hang on a minute,' said Eromanga, 'I just might need a little in me pocket just in case I meet up with…arr, never mind, you know what I'm talking about.' Eromanga grabbed a hand full of notes and stashed them in his pocket. He picked up his beer and placed the edge of his glass on his lip to down the lot in one swoop. He placed his glass on the bar. 'I'll just get me gear up to me room and be back quicker than a split flash o' lightnin',' he said.

Eromanga returned to the bar and began to drink while he chatted with some of the regulars.

Around late afternoon, a few newcomers arrived. A counter dinner was available. The menu was 'Irish stew', 'bangers and mash', 'steak and eggs with chips'. Eromanga treated himself to the steak.

An extra waitress came on duty at dinner time. She was a pretty brunette, wore a black mini skirt, white blouse and high-heel shoes. A nametag pinned on her blouse read, 'Ellie'.

She took Eromanga's plate when he had finished. 'How'd you enjoy your meal?' she asked.

'Sure beats kangaroo stew,' he answered.

Ellie giggled. 'Surely that's not all you eat?'

Eromanga looked her in the eye and said,' Just between you and me Ellie m'dear, every now and then I treat meself to a bit of mutton.' He gave her a wink. She smiled and walked off. Eromanga gaped at her shapely legs and gave a sigh.

The time was approaching 10pm. Al, the barman made an announcement. 'All right everybody, order up your last drinks. We'll be closing up in six minutes.'

'What's goin' on Al?' Eromanga asked. 'Don't we just close the doors, turn out the lights and stay here as long as we like?'

'That's the way it used to be,' said Al. 'I'm sorry to say those days are over.'

'Fair crack o' the whip Al! There's got to be a reason.'

'There's a reason all right,' Di interrupted. 'There's a new cop in town and she's after a few stripes.'

'What, a woman copper here in this neck of the woods!' Eromanga exclaimed. 'That's right,' Di replied. 'Dickless Tracy, they call her. She's an absolute B-I-T-C-H.'

'Di is dead right Eromanga,' Al said. 'You can set your watch by her. She'll show up here at one minute past ten. You can bet your lefty.'

'Ah well,' said Eromanga. 'I'd better drink up. Maybe an early night will do me good.'

After taking a shower in the guests' bathroom, Eromanga retired to his room. All he was wearing was a pair of tartan boxer shorts. He was about to get into bed when he heard a knock on the veranda door. He opened it to see Di standing there, clad only in a see-through nylon nightie. He gawked at her for a moment and said, 'Hello Diane, what can I do for you?'

'I thought I'd say goodnight seeing I am right next door and you're here all alone.'

'That's mighty nice of you. Coming in for a bit?'

'What do you mean, a bit?' Di giggled as she entered the room and sat herself down on the side of the bed.

'Heh heh. That could mean a number of things I guess,' Eromanga answered with a grin.

'Yes it could.' Di pressed on the bed mattress causing it to move up and down. 'I thought you might be in the mood for a bit of 'you know what', if you get my drift.' Di pouted her lips, giving a sexy smile.

'I see,' Eromanga said. 'Well maybe I would, maybe I wouldn't. What's the catch?'

'There's no catch. Don't tell me you're not up to it.'

'I ain't been with a woman for quite a while Di but I reckon I can still manage. Heh heh.'

'That's good. Now what did you have in mind of doing with that fist full of dollars I saw you pluck from your biscuit tin?'

'Aha! I thought as much. You're more interested in me money than you are in giving me a bit of pleasure, aren't ya?'

'I wouldn't be wanting all of it Eromanga, just a little at a time. I'm happy to make it stretch out for as long as you are here.'

Eromanga looked Di in the eye and grinned. 'What the hell! What have I got to lose?' He closed the latch on the veranda door. Sometime later as Di lay on the bed beside Eromanga, she took hold of his hand and said, 'That was truly out of this world. How about we have some more of that action in the morning? I don't have to start till ten.' Eromanga did not reply. He was sound asleep.

Later the following day, Eromanga did a stroll up town and back, which was not all that long. He believed in doing a little exercise every day before lining up at the bar. He indulged in a few drinks with a regular customer named Barry Thompson who was generally known as 'Tommo'

Tommo was shortish, freckly and weak looking. He challenged Eromanga to a game of snooker to which he agreed. Eromanga had not played for some time but he had a good eye and, as Tommo soon discovered, he was hard to beat.

After losing three games in a row, Tommo placed his cue in a rack and said, 'Thanks cobber. That'll do me.'

'Thanks Tommo. Guess I got lucky.' Eromanga replied. They had been sipping cold beer the entire time they were playing while in the background country music played including Slim Dusty's *I'd Love to Have a Beer with Duncan*.

During their last game a drifter named Eddie Wise came in. He bought a cold beer and watched them play. Eddie was tall, slim and well dressed. He wore a dark blue suit and blue suede shoes. His hair was fair and brushed back.

He took the opportunity to ask Eromanga for a game. He suggested five dollars go to the winner. Eromanga accepted and was soon five dollars richer. 'You were a bit lucky there,' Eddie said. 'How about giving me a chance to win my money back?'

'Sure.' Eromanga agreed and once again he pocketed a five-dollar note.

'Damn!' Eddie cursed. 'It can't happen three times in a row. I'm starting to get my eye in. How about one more game?'

'It's your money you're losing Eddie. Why not?'

'Okay. I think I've got the angles down pat now. How about we make it interesting and play for one hundred bucks?'

Eromanga took a swig of beer. 'Like I said Eddie, it's your money you're losing. You're on.'

Eromanga took first shot and almost potted a red. Eddie followed and cleaned up the table. 'Ha ha. I told you I got my eye in. That's a hundred bucks you owe me. Hand it over.'

Eromanga emptied his pockets, handed Eddie four twenties and two tens. All he had left were the two fives he had won earlier plus a bit of loose change.

'Thanks mate,' Eddie said.' Don't want another go at winning your money back eh?'

'Go to hell, you hustler.' Eromanga snarled as he walked back to the bar. 'Give me another drink Al.'

Eddie left the building.

A week and a half later Eromanga sat at the bar chatting with Tommo and sometimes Al and Di.

Al said to Eromanga, 'You'd better make the most of the rest of the day mate.'

'What are you getting at Al?'

'I'm afraid you'll have to be on your way tomorrow. Your cash supply is just about exhausted. There's just enough left to see you on your way.'

'Crikey! Are you sure? That seemed to go a bit quick.'

'You're not doubting me, are you? That 'Down down, prices are down,' they keep ramming down our throats is nothing but a load of bunk. If anything, it should be 'Up, up, prices are up'. Sorry Pal, that's the way it is.'

'Gawd! I'll just have to take your word for it Al. I was really enjoying me stay.' Eromanga gave Di a wink.

She smiled her cutest smile and mouthed the words, 'One more night' at him.

That night after 10pm Di came to Eromanga's room. 'Sorry Di,' he said. 'I hate to tell you but I'm just about all out of moolah.'

'Don't worry lover boy. Tonight's on me. Consider it a bonus if you like 'cause that's the way I'm gonna look at it. You are something special Eromanga. I'm really gonna miss you.'

'Them's the nicest words I've heard in a long time.' Eromanga said. Di kissed him.

The following morning Eromanga packed his port and an Esky filled with beer stubbies into the Jeep. He bid goodbye to his friends and got started on the long dusty trip homeward, drinking steadily all the way.

The dogs heard the Jeep as it approached the hut. They all ran down to meet it barking excitedly all the way up beside the barbed wire fence where Eromanga brought the vehicle to an abrupt stop.

He was quite intoxicated by then. Instead of going through the fence gate, he attempted to get through the taut barbed wire.

In his drunken stupor, he cut himself in several places while his excited hounds jumped upon him. He began to bleed. The hungry hounds began to lick his blood as he struggled to free himself from the prickly barbs.

They really loved their master.

Two days later station manager Jackson Tully, was doing an inspection of the property in a short wheel based Land Rover.

With him was attractive Marjorie Mulcahy, a jillaroo. 'I have the same initials as Marilyn Monroe,' she would say. She was every bit as curvaceous. She liked to wear tight jeans and checked shirts of which she would usually leave the top three buttons undone. Jackson often got her to do the rounds with him.

'We might drive by Eromanga's hut,' he said. 'He may not be back yet.'

'Are you thinking what I think you're thinking?' Marjorie asked with a gleam in her eye.

Jackson gave a chuckle. 'Great minds think alike,' he said.

'Those dogs of his will sure be missing him,' Marjorie said. 'He sure loves them.'

'And they love him just as much my sweet.'

They approached the paddock where the hut stood and saw it in the distance.

'Looks like he's home. There's the Jeep.' Jackson said, sounding a little disappointed. They continued to drive to the hut.

What they saw upon their arrival put them into a state of disbelief.

There were Eromanga's dogs by the fence, standing near the remains of their master, a mixture of torn clothing and sun-baked flesh.

His beloved hounds had devoured him.

Ray Ray stood closest to him, wagging his tail.

LAST MOMENTS

Bakthi Ross

A loud thud! Everyone moved in their seats and their heads lifted up and listened to the voice of the plane's captain. The voice sounded confident, not revealing any fear to upset the passengers. The captain said, 'Engine failure, please stay calm. We are doing everything we possibly can to land quickly.' Everyone was asked to put on the life jackets. Passengers were looking at each other with helpless expressions. Some were praying and some wrote things on paper and put the notes in plastic bags. Some called to God and pleaded for help. Others sent messages on their iPhones.

Emily was one of the passengers, travelling with her two-year-old daughter. She did not know how to handle the situation. She looked at her daughter, Casey. The innocent eyes of her child made her cry. Casey didn't know what was going on. Everyone was facing death but her daughter was happy, playing and laughing. *I wish I was a child. I would not have to face the fear of death. Being a child is a good thing*, thought Emily. She put on the baby sling and held Casey closer to her heart. Emily thought, *if my daughter and I are killed in a plane crash, my husband will be alone.* She took pictures of the situation and sent an email to her husband.

'My last moments,' she said

She prayed. My plea, Dear God, please help us. My child had not experienced life yet.

Many passengers were thinking of God and asking for help. Some said, 'I do not even believe in God, but I am asking for His help.'

An old man had a heart attack. He was left on the seat without anyone helping him.

The plane was moving violently. Everyone had lost hope. No one worried about their luggage or anything. Facing death created a new mental state. All worries of life suddenly disappeared out of their minds.

They were feeling for their families and wanted to be closer to them. This sudden change in their life situation made them feel they loved them dearly. They wanted to say 'I love you' to their families but were not given that chance in their last moments.

One of the passengers opened up the Bible and started to pray. Others did something to overcome their last moments of facing death. One of the passengers, a businessman, stood still like a stone. He was frozen by his fear of death.

The passengers could see one of the engines was on fire. Emily thought, *we are going to be burnt to death.*

Some were shaken, others cried uncontrollably.

Emily looked at the passengers. A shocked atmosphere was expressed by their behaviours. Some made peace with themselves; others were reluctant to leave the world and were angry and frustrated.

Emily's thoughts were going wild. She was thinking of all sorts of things. As adults we still do not know how to handle our last moments. Her daughter was only two-years old and her mental state was unchanged. She behaved normally. *Would it be better if the captain did not tell us the situation of the plane? Could we prepare for the situation more effectively and stay calm like a child?*

Her thoughts were erratic. She was thinking about what her husband would do if she and her child were killed in a plane crash. Tears rolled down her face as she thought of his sadness. She had accepted her death, feeling only the pain her husband would go through.

She wanted to be with him and hug him. She stopped worrying about herself and her daughter. Our minds work differently when we face death.

She kissed her daughter many times and cried. *Why do we cry when we face death,* she thought? *Is it the fear of death or the pain we are going to suffer during death? Why does dying create sadness?*

It is as if we have some connection with each other. When someone dies some things will break away from us. Life is like an electrical current running through us. When the current is cut off we feel it. Like electrical circuits, we emit heat, reflect light and electrical vibes. That is why we feel death. We are in a vibes of an electrical circuit of life, planets and the atmosphere. Everything is interconnected.

Emily's mind wandered onto something else. She was thinking, *I wonder if I could save my daughter? She is only a baby. Can God be that cruel?*

One of passengers took out a piece of paper and wrote down his name and phone number and asked, 'If anyone survives please phone this number and tell them I love them.'

Everyone was going through an emotional rollercoaster. Panic and helplessness pervaded the scene. Some died before the crash because they couldn't handle the stress. They took an early exit by having heart attacks.

One woman cried out loud and carried on. Others tried to calm her down but she would not listen. The air hostesses could not get off theirs seats to help anyone. Emily was thinking about her afterlife.

When we die our bodies will go cold. The heat disappears and the electrical vibes disappear into the atmosphere. *Will I reincarnate?* thought Emily. *What if I could come back in another life to see my husband?*

Without light there is no life. Our electrical vibes are in other lives or in the atmosphere. Does electricity really die or just disappear into the atmosphere? Life is not eternal life but electricity may be. It could travel to heaven and hell. *Oh, no,* Emily thought, *I could go to hell, if I die today. I haven't been to confession for a long time. My sins, my sins, I do not want to think about it.*

She shuts off her mind.

Another violent movement shook people in their seats. Some were thrown off the seats and hit the walls of the plane. Blood was everywhere. Emily closed her daughter's eyes. She did not want her to see it. Bodies lay on the floor. Seeing their last moments made her cry again.

The people were like children crying for help. Many were on their knees pleading to God. Seeing death for the first time, Emily realised life could end at any moment.

When you are living you do not fear death much, but when you encounter situations like this, you value your life as precious. Her deranged mumbled thoughts kept her hanging on to Casey and her life. She could not move her hands or legs and was frozen with fear of death.

Death! End of my life. I will no longer exist. I have not done all the things I wanted to do. My life is going to be interrupted. I did not have a plan. I lived my life as though I am going to reach retirement and will see my grandchildren live. I had a retirement plan but I did not plan for this. I am feeling the presence of death and finding it difficult to breathe.

The feeling was indescribable. *If I survive will I stop travelling or can I cope with another situation like this?*

With every movement of the plane Emily held her daughter close. It was like hell. People were screaming and dying. The dead body of a woman revealed her eyes were wide open, staring into space. *If I could get off my seat I could close her eyes but I cannot.* Emily felt as if the dead woman was asking for help.

Half the passengers were dead or injured and some were mourning with pain. Emily was still alive but scared to look around. Her thoughts came to an end. She couldn't think or talk anymore.

Why are endings filled with silence and quietness? A sudden quietness filled the plane's atmosphere. The plane's door broke open. Some flew out. Others clung to the seats.

With a loud noise, the plane broke into pieces. Emily was still tied to the seat, holding on to Casey. She flew in the wind rolling many times over. She still held Casey tight. She could have let go of her many times with the strong wind fighting her. It was painful to breathe. She did not let Casey absorb much air. She covered her nose with her hand. *The fall to my death*, she thought.

Previously Emily had control over many things in her life and was at peace. Now she had no control over anything. Nature took over her life. She flew without a parachute and had no control over her flight. She moved according to wind pressure. It took a while.

Finally she landed on the sea still in the plane seat. Emily was floating on the middle of the sea. Bodies fell around her. Emily and Casey had to fight the sea to survive. The plane seat floated on the sea thanks to plastic and foam on the seat.

They floated aimlessly. They were both wet and cold. She had the phone in her pocket and called her husband, but she didn't know where she was. Sea all around her, no landscapes to identify where she was.

She was convinced if she had to face the night on the ocean she would definitely die. Eight hours later, helicopters circled the sky. She screamed and waved her hands. Finally, they rescued her. She was alive.

After what she had been through, and with her fear of death lingering, Emily did not enjoy her escape. She was still cautious. She was given a hot cup of tea and a blanket to wrap around herself. Emily and her child were safe and warm.

Finally they were driven to their home. The first thing she did was give her husband a big hug. Tears rolled down her face. She felt the sense of relief but an unhealed pain still tormented her.

The next day Emily woke up early and looked around the house. She felt the importance of life. She was a changed person. She took some of her art works and threw them away. 'Not worth doing,' she said to herself.

Now she wanted to do the things that were meaningful. She wanted to live her life fully and not worry about material things. She wanted to help people and save the world. Facing the prospect of death changed her mentality. From death to life. Omega to Alpha.

A MATTER OF TRUST

Margaret Taylor

'HAVE you ever wondered what Gerry is hiding behind that huge wall around his property?'

'It's none of our business Ellen,' Anthony answered.

'But it could be anything. You must admit it's odd that no-one on the estate has ever been invited into his house. So what's the big secret? Steve Collins said he'd heard Gerry wouldn't let anyone on his property because of contamination. What does that mean? Has he got a crop of marijuana growing there? Is he a drug dealer, a people smuggler? What? What does he do?'

Anthony sighed and looked up from his computer. He was a patient man, in his mid-thirties, trim, well groomed, used to being tested. 'Don't be ridiculous Ellen; you're letting your imagination run away with you. Gerry is running a business, like everyone else on the estate. What's more he's the manager so he'd hardly be doing anything illegal, would he?'

Ellen pursed her lips but did not respond.

'Think about it,' Anthony said. 'Gerry has his reputation to consider. Have you forgotten that a condition of coming onto the estate was to respect other's privacy'? It's a matter of trust that we abide by that agreement.'

Ellen rolled her eyes and shrugged.

Anthony looked over the top of his glasses at his wife and thought back to the advertisement in a national newspaper which had brought them to their present circumstances.

He recalled the wording: *We are inviting independent, enterprising people to join our community. This is a once in a lifetime opportunity to design your own home and start a business within a privately owned estate. All applications will be treated with respect and consideration. Successful applicants will be assisted in applying for a business grant and mortgage. For further information please contact the manager.*

Anthony had contacted the manager and was impressed with the package, but Ellen had commented, 'Sounds too good to be true.'

However, it was a genuine offer, which they took, and started their business designing and making women's clothes for formal occasions. The garments were exclusive designs and through hard work their clientele base was steadily growing. Ellen, being a tall willowy redhead, captured the elegance and understated simplicity of the designs. Photos of Ellen modelling the creations were on their website, *Anton*.

All twenty properties on the estate were on acreage; on private land, all small businesses run from home. Anthony and Ellen had been part of the community for three years.

Residents occasionally got together for parties. There was gossip about the parties, especially those held on Sam's property.

Sam, dark unruly hair, tanned, athletic build, single, a loner with a charismatic personality, was everyone's favourite party host. He was known as Sam, Sam, the Ladies Man, but rumour was that he was anyone's man. People made guesses about his background but no-one knew for sure where he came from or what his business was. Sam liked it that way, calling himself an entrepreneur. Sam liked to keep people guessing. It was part of the mystique he cultivated.

It was after an invitation to one of Sam's parties that the argument began.

'Oh come on Anthony, don't be such a pain, let's go to the party.'

Anthony shook his head. He was at his desk working on orders. Sitting back in his chair and stretching, he replied, 'You know I don't like parties. You know I don't like Sam. So why ask me?'

Ellen went over to her husband and put her arms around his shoulders. She ruffled his wiry brown hair, noticing a few grey hairs. 'You're working too hard love, you look tired,' she said softly. 'A break will do you good, help you to relax. James and Sarah are going. You like them.'

'Yes, but I don't want to be in Sam's house. I can't stand the man. I always have the feeling he's up to something.'

'Oh, for heaven's sake, just because he's single and attractive doesn't...'

'So you find him attractive do you?' Anthony swung around to face Ellen. 'Is that why you want to go to the party?'

'Don't be so silly! You sound like a jealous teenager. Grow up Anthony.' She backed away and putting her hands on her hips leaned towards him. 'You know what, you're becoming boring. It's all work, work, and more work with you.'

'Oh, boring am I?' Anthony stood up and pushed the chair away with the back of his foot. The chair scooted on the tiled floor to the other side of the room where it hit the wall and stopped. 'I think you're forgetting that without boring old me there'd be no business and we wouldn't be living here.'

Ellen stepped forward and put her hand on his arm.

He brushed her hand off and turned to walk away. 'Oh do what you want Ellen,' he said over his shoulder. 'You always do anyway.'

Ellen went alone to the party.

She arrived home in the early hours of the following morning after a few too many glasses of wine – only the best wine because no expense was spared when it came to Sam's parties and his guests.

Anthony heard Ellen enter their bedroom but did not move.

She flopped down on the bed beside him. 'I know you're only pretending to be asleep.' She planted a kiss on Anthony's cheek and whispered, 'Have you forgiven me for going to the party?'

Anthony pushed back the covers, sat up and looked at his wife. Her thick, lustrous, auburn hair fell in loose curls around her bare shoulders. She was wearing their latest creation, a full-length silk fitted gown with narrow straps. The emerald earrings, an anniversary gift, complemented the emerald green of her dress. She had that look in her eye which he found hard to resist. But he tried.

'Well?' asked Ellen.

'Well what?'

'Am I forgiven? I hope so because I've brought you a souvenir. Something we can share and enjoy together.'

Anthony hoped it was what he was thinking.

'First of all', Ellen began, 'you'll never guess what happened tonight.'

Anthony's heart sank. 'I don't think I want to know.'

'You'll love it when I tell you.' Ellen's eyes were gleaming mischievously.

Anthony began to feel nervous.

'I've found out what Gerry's business is, and it's not what people think.'

Anthony heard warning bells. 'How did you find out?'

Ellen was so hyped up she did not notice the concern on Anthony's face.

'Sam dared me to climb over the wall of Gerry's property.'

'Oh no.' Anthony groaned putting his head in his hands. 'I might have known he'd be involved. What were you thinking?'

Ellen smirked, 'Oh come on Anthony. It was just a bit of fun.'

'A bit of fun? Do you realise we could lose everything if Gerry finds out you've been on his property? Did he see you?'

'No, no, no.' Ellen laughed. She stood up, swaying a little, her hands behind her back. 'Guess what I've got.'

Anthony was too worried to care. 'No idea. I give up.'

Ellen looked triumphant as she brought both hands from behind her back and held the object in her cupped hands, like an offering.

Anthony looked blank. 'It's an apple.'

'Yes, but this is no ordinary apple.' Ellen said, dangling it by the stalk.

'Looks like an ordinary apple to me.'

'Ah ha, well you're wrong. THIS,' she said, holding the apple in her hand as if it were a delicate piece of porcelain, 'is one of Gerry's specials. THIS is his business. Gerry has created a new breed of apple. He sells them exclusively to high-end restaurants and small businesses who sell organic food and products.'

Anthony was staring at Ellen, not saying a word.

She continued. 'When Sam dared me to climb over the wall I accepted the dare. To prove I had been there I picked an apple and took it back to him'. Ellen smiled at Anthony. 'And this, my darling, is THE apple.'

Anthony was still staring at Ellen, but this time his mouth had dropped open in disbelief.

Ellen sat down on the bed. 'Close your mouth Anthony,' she said putting her finger on his lips. 'Are you surprised, now you know what Gerry's business is? Disappointed it's not something we can all gossip about?'

Anthony jumped out of bed. 'Are you crazy? If Gerry finds out about this we'll be forced to leave the estate. You know the rules Ellen, one of which is NOT to go onto Gerry's property.'

'Oh damn Gerry, and damn you,' Ellen shouted. 'It's only an apple.'

When she saw the look on Anthony's face Ellen changed tactics. She moved in close, very close, to Anthony and smiled the seductive smile she knew he found hard to resist. She put her hand on the back of his neck, gently massaging away the tension. When he began to relax she brought the apple from behind her back and held it to Anthony's lips. She looked into his eyes and slowly licked the apple. 'It's just a bite of an apple Anthony. It won't be the end of the world.'

But it was the end of the world as Anthony and Ellen knew it.

It was, in fact, the beginning of the end.

The Pulse of Life

Vera Murray

I put my finger on the pulse of life.
It pounds with vibrating movement;
Of joyous life, of hell torment;

And all the music of the world,
Resounds within the echoing places,
Of my soul,

And dream-like visions of great things,
Float before my searching mind.

THE AUTHORS

Kasper J. Beaumont was born and raised in Australia and lives a quiet life with the family in a seaside town. Combining a love of fantasy and a penchant for travel in the Hunters of Reloria trilogy, Kasper started to write on the urging of friends and family and enjoys watching readers become immersed in the magical world of Reloria. Kasper is a pen name for a rather shy author who is happy to remain unnamed.

Judy Boyd re-entered the workforce as a Community Mental Health Nurse after a failed attempt at retirement, aged sixty-eight...great for six months but what do I do now? Over the next sixteen years she learnt life's important lessons – knowledge does not equal wisdom, humility is a virtue and a writing life is a good alternative to a working life. At eighty-two, having cracked the code of successful retirement she has turned her attention to the challenge of writing competitions and loves her life as an octogenarian, contract-bridge playing cougar who likes to write.

Kelly Brettell is married with three wonderful children. She works in libraries and is studying a Bachelor of Creative Industries majoring in Creative and Professional Writing. Her passion is and always has been writing. Kelly writes to feel, touch and connect. *The Diamond Key* is dedicated to her family, her brothers, parents and niece.

Santina Cardillo is a mother of two and has lived in Greater Brisbane all of her life, the last 10 years in the Moreton Bay District. She has only recently reignited her childhood passion for writing. Her heritage is Sicilian and family is very important and provides her with ample inspiration. She is also interested in spiritualism, mysticism and nature. Tina is currently working on self-publishing a collection of poems, titled *A Pocket Full of Faith, Hope and Love.*

Suzanne Cowell has lived in Strathpine in Pine Rivers district with her husband since 1971. From the age of thirteen she has always envisaged herself as a writer. Persistence has kept her dream alive. After raising two daughters, she now devotes her time to following her passion of writing. She is a co-founder of the Strathpine Writers' Group, which began in 2009. Her poems and short stories have been published in the Arana Writers' and Arts Alliance anthologies.

Phil Devine was born and bred in the northern suburbs of Brisbane in the mid-fifties when much of it was still largely bushland. He inherited a love of science, nature and reading from his father. He moved to Alice Springs in Central Australia in the late nineties, where he lives quite happily with his two dogs in a caravan and annexe on a rural block. He wanted to see the real Outback before they built a car park over it. He continues to live there avoiding macadam as much as possible. Interests include bush walking, photography, reading and, yes, star gazing. A great lover of tradition and innovation, he has no problems whatsoever with the apparent dichotomy inherent in that.

Bernie Dowling is a Pine Rivers journalist and author. His books include fiction and non-fiction. His latest works are the musical play *Dagworth Day,* (with Gloria Swenson), another musical *Christian and Humble,* and his first novel, *Iraqi Icicle.* His neo-noir detective Steele Hill returns for this anthology and his life is on the (laughter) line. Again.

Daphne Gibson has been writing poetry from an early age. She has been successful in attaining first prizes in a number of literary contests. Her first publication was in the Brisbane Girls' Grammar School Year Book. Daphne has given writing workshops for both adults and children. Her work includes short stories, children's stories and articles. Poetry is her first love.

Maurice Hardy is a musician and song writer in the country genre. Recovering from a serious illness, he wrote a 95,000 word novel *Shadows of Perfection*. He is seeking a publisher. Maurice's story for this anthology continues his fascination with the interplay of nature and families.

Ronald Holt retired from the Queensland public sector in 2006 after more than forty years' service – the last 14 years in the Office of Fair Trading. He wrote numerous reports and departmental correspondence on a wide range of issues and is now applying those skills to his love of creative writing. He has edited four anthologies, 2007, 2009, 2011 and 2013 for the Arana Writers' Group. He has had short stories published on Anzac Cove and global warming.

Belinda Janz has written short stories, poetry and stories for children as well as assisting in writing a radio play. She has won short-story competitions and has been published in Australia and overseas in magazines and anthologies. Her other interests include sewing, craft work, ancient history studies, cooking, reading, spirituality, massage and helping people.

David MacLaughlin began writing for a staff magazine when he came fourth from world-wide entries for a travel article. Writing took a back seat as David became active in choral and Celtic choirs and musical theatre. After that it was time to give writing its proper priority in things cultural. As a member of Arana Writers' Group, David has contributed to the group's anthologies with articles factual, humorous, some fiction and travel tales.

Vera Murray was born in Allora, Queensland. She has been writing since her school days. She is a former Pine Rivers Shire Councillor. She has edited a magazine overseas. While running the Writer's Circle group in Pine Rivers, she edited and published three anthologies. Her book *Move Over James Bond and Other Stories* and her first novel *Leap Year: Blood Lust* were recently published. Her latest book *Move Over plus Humorous Verses* was released on 2014.

Anne Olsson is a remedial therapist living and working in Pine Rivers. She has been an enthusiastic actor on the amateur stage and, in recent years, an eager world traveller. Her poetry and articles have been published in newspapers and magazines.

R. William Penshorn has travelled the world but still calls Australia home. Now retired and still touring, he spent most of his working years involved in surveying and civil engineering projects. He has written several movie scripts. His interests include comic collecting, classic automobiles, rock 'n' roll, art, surfing, and, of course, writing. His Tonka Toys were on display in the Queensland Museum's *Collectorama*, which ended in March 2014.

Bakthi Ross is a member of the Caboolture Writer's Link. She started writing because of a dream and has written many children's books. Her ebooks are available at www.appspublisher.com. A mother of two children, she lives at Morayfield in Moreton Bay Region.

Sue Sander lives in Moreton Bay Region and is married with two children. She loves writing in her spare time between working and caring for her family. Short stories are her favourite genre and she hopes to one day write a novel. Sue loves words and the images and feelings a writer can create with a beautifully crafted sentence.

Jane Sharp settled in the Pine Rivers area in 1994. She has always loved reading and writing as a form of relaxation. Now that her family have grown and left the nest she has more time to devote to her favourite past-time. Jane is the author of the *Vision* psychic detective series, available as eBooks through Amazon and other online shops.

Margaret Taylor was born many moons ago in England. She has lived in the North of England, the South of England, America and New Zealand. She currently lives in Brisbane, Australia, with her family. She writes when she remembers to, and reads a lot of books because she is in a book club. Margaret is retired from the workforce but not from life or a challenge.

Paimarire Teague has always found herself drawn towards the creative arts. She is still on the journey to find herself and would like her future to involve something to do with writing. Paimarire has always felt that writing was a way to release any emotions that she felt she could not express to anybody else without causing lasting damage to herself or those who matter to her. Paimarire's temporary goal is to graduate high school with at least a B average. She partakes in drama and dance classes and also enjoys art.

Tatiana Werle-Bertling is a teenage girl who grew up in the Moreton Bay Region. She reads books by the bazillion and her parents are always sighing over how every available inch of shelving is always stuffed with…books! It was just sort've natural that she started writing her memoirs and short stories in her free time. She is considering doing a little writing in future – not entirely sure yet.

Sarah L. Wilson is 16-years-old and has been stubbornly insisting she would be an author from quite a young age. She has written mostly drafts of books and short stories, although she has nothing against a good play or poem. Her other interests include reading, theatre, music, science and the internet.

Phone 617 3264 2311
Email peter@petercampbellrealty.com
Web www.petercampbellrealty.com

THE ILLUSTRATORS

KEN ARMSTRONG studied at the Dundee College of Art in Scotland before pursuing a diverse career path in illustration, journalism, script writing, magazine editing, and photography, not to mention a number of years in the UK military. Ken is at home with drawing, painting (mostly in oils) and has embraced digital art. His landscapes and portraits are in several private collections and his pastel portraits have proved very popular. He was the inaugural president of the Arts Alliance of Pine Rivers. He returned to presidential office this year.

RUSSELL BROWN is an Australian newspaper and artistic photographer. He has had exhibitions in Australia and overseas. Russell's work was included in the *Salon de la Photo* exhibition in Paris. He is the author of two books and supplied the cover image for the Bernie Dowling novel *Iraqi Icicle*. Visit http://www.russbrownart.com

BRAD COOPER is a professional photographer from the Moreton Bay Region of Australia.

CHRIS HIGGINS is a professional photographer from the Moreton Bay Region of Australia.

JAKI MARTINEZ and **MIKE FERTIG** are a young designing team from the US.

VERA MURRAY is an amateur artist as well as a writer.

VISIT www.bentbananabooks.com